Sea-Quences

Sea-Quences

Blue Water Sailing Adventures

Captain Al A. Adams

To order additional copies of this book, contact:
Xlibris Corporation
1-888-795-4274
www.Xlibris.com
Orders@Xlibris.com
26122

CONTENTS

About the Author   vii
Dedication   xi
Further Appreciation   xiii
Acknowledgements   xv
Photo Index to Vessels   xvii
About the Cover Photo   xix

Preface   1

"Skipper, Are We Going to Make it?"   7
    Chapter 1: Thorough Misery   9
    Chapter 2: "The Finest Yacht In The World" . . . ? 23
    Chapter 3: A Furious World   39
    Chapter 4: So This Is Yachting   45
    Chapter 5: Answers   69

White Death Came Bumping   75

When It All Happens   145

Editor's Acknowledgements   159

Glossary of Terms   161

About the Author

Captain Al A. Adams always said, "See the world before you leave it." That he did—and is still doing. Al is a world traveler, avid sailor in both racing and cruising—a pioneer of yacht deliveries and Marine Surveying. He began sailing in 1929 and has logged over 346,000 miles on the open sea. He owned and operated the first Sailing School on the West Coast. He is a Marine Surveyor of 56 years, Lecturer and Writer. He had been the Sailing Coach for Cal Tech University. Al was the Sailing Master in three Transpacific Yacht Races and the Acapulco race. In 1959 he placed 1st in his class aboard *"Echo"*. He created the prestigious "Al Adams & Son Perpetual Trophy" which was coveted by Yacht Clubs all along the Pacific Coast to Oregon. Al was commissioned by many "world class" individuals to skipper their fine yachts throughout the world. The ensuing adventures from these travels are a must-read for anyone who prefers more than the usual story! He skippered fine yachts, such as Herreshoff's *Vayu* and *Queen Mab*. Some of the other fine yachts were *Tamarit*, *Enchantress, Dwyn Wen, Stella Maris II, Cotton Blossom, San Souci, Nam Sang*, Finistere and many more. He has received the "Seaman of the Year Award" as well as the "Boatman of the Year Award". Al is also the recipient of the United States Coast Guard's "A" Award, the highest award a civilian may receive. Al received this commendation for risking his life to tow a blazing cruiser, away from San

Pedro's Cerritos Channel Marinas, thus saving yachts worth millions of dollars. He towed it toward the fire boats after pulling the owner from the water. At this time, Al was also nominated for the U. S. Treasury Department's Life-Saving Medal. Al filmed his voyages and some were subsequently shown on the Jack Douglas series "I Search for Adventure" and "Golden Voyage". Al was a member of a scientific expedition to Ambrim Island, New Hebrides to the erupting Marum volcanoe. He has paddled a dugout canoe down the Sepik River in New Guinea, sailed the Japanese Islands from Hokaido to Hiroshima, sailed the Philippine Islands by dugout and outrigger. Al sailed Lake Titicaca, the world's highest navigatable lake, cruised Islands of the Kingdom of Tonga—Vavau, Haapai and Tongatapu. He carried the first Expedition Flag to be signed by a King. Al cruised the Aegean, Adriatic, Mediterranean, Cyclades Islands, the Coasts of Turkey, Yugoslavia, Greece, Italy and the Coast of Albania. He has also safaried in Africa, New Britain and in New Guinea. He skippered his own yacht, "Southwind" from California to Panama, Florida, South America, through the West Indies and back to California over a year and a half period. He and his wife, Dianne, were guests on the final cruise of the "Queen Mary" when she rounded Cape Horn and retired in Long Beach. Al was Commodore of the Cabrillo Beach Yacht Club in San Pedro and the Southwind Yacht Club in Wilmington, California. From his extensive travels, Al has acquired one of the largest burgee collections, by an individual, in the world. During these sailing years, Al also wrote for various publications and newspapers including; The Sea Magazine (Associate Editor), The Yachting News, Yachting, Pacific Motorboat, Rudder, The Sportsman, The Adventurerers' Club News, The Douglas Airview during his 12 years of employment with Douglas Aircraft in Santa Monica. During that time, he was a member of the Public Relations Department of Douglas Aircraft Company, Incorporated. In 1972, Al was the President of the Adventurer's Club of Los Angeles. He is still currently a member of the Adventurer's Club of Los Angeles, the Explorer's Club of New York, and the Kiwanis Club.

Thousands of people have learned to sail from Captain Al Adams, both through his Sailing School and through private commission for special events. Al has worked with many celebrities and famous people such as: Bing Crosby, Julie Andrews, William Conrad, Walter Cronkite, and Gene Hackman.

Dedication

There are not enough ways to show devotion and affection to the one who shares my world. Seek ways to elevate her with praise? Perhaps. She went to the ends of the earth with me—the least I can do is recognize the spirit she provides for our endeavors.

To Dianne this book is dedicated.

Further Appreciation

My thanks to my son Dale. He was always there, a part of the sailing scene. He grew up on the decks of the yachts. He came on the boating picture while I was Captain of the 136 foot grand schooner *Enchantress*, one of the finest. He learned to walk on board, so his position during his early months was in his playpen and jump-swing, a few feet forward of the helm and binnacle so I could keep track of him while sailing the big schooner. In this position he could observe and learn. Later, I opened my Sailing School and he attended many classes. He grew up learning the basics and fundamentals at the right age. As a result, he is a fine boatman of sail and power yachts.

My mother and father approved that I was intent in my sailing and from a hobby I wished to make it a big part of my profession. They played a big part in aiding me to proceed. Never were they against my intentions.

Acknowledgements

Helpful attitudes of this group. Every aid was thought-filled. There were tireless suggestions from my wife, Dianne, and editorial guidance by professional Michelle Rush. My gratitude to my brother Ervin and his wife, Lois Adams, Roberta Adams, Thomas G. Skahill, Dick Brownell, Tom and Irene Clint, Jason Hailey and Gretalee, Gary Mortimer and Marcelle, Sam and Pat Franco, Jay Rush, Steve Waterford, Bill Fields, Ron and Arlynn Stark, Don Clothier and Chris, William O. Muff, Ted Williams, Henry Kehler, Dick Kelty, Max Hurlbut and Hueih Hueih, Sven F. W. Wahlroos and Eva, Robert Gilliland, Max Ramsey and Gwen, Jack Owen, Bob Wright, Paul Kopp and Mary, my son Dale Adams and Sylvia Robinson, my grandson Dale Douglas Adams, Roy Roush, Keith H. Chase and Lynn, Tom Mooneyham, Angela Boland, David Miller, Robert Aronoff, Robert C. Williams, Frank Haigler, Wallace Bagley and Jane L. Lovein, my faithful cousin. Hilda Dullam Serr has given me endless aid over a period of more than sixty years in my journalistic endeavors, culminating in this book.

Photo Index to Vessels

Coast Guard Cutter	*60, 61*
Dwyn Wen	*29*
Enchantress	*27*
Morning Star	*27*
Parismina	*120, 121*
PBM Flying Boat	*54, 55*
Queen Mab	*70*
Shearwater	*76*
Sun Yat Sen	*52*
Stella Maris II	*146*
Tamarit	*77, 80, 111, 139, 141, 142, 143*
Vayu	*8, 19, 35, 42, 46, 57, 61, 67*

About the Cover Photo

Steve Waterford, Photographer

Being a member of The Adventurers' Club of Los Angeles has allowed me to associate with others who like adventure—any kind of real adventure. The club meets once a week, with a scheduled program, allowing the membership to gather and share their vast experiences.

My minds-eye has seen and stored away that which I needed. I walked into my home, scanned the table and desk tops. There it was—the cover photo of the sea in action on the Adventurers' Club News, addressing the "Night of High Adventure" as it so professionally was captured by Steve Waterford's eye and lens—and in color and action—if only Steve's permission could be secured in Florida for my use of his artful ability. My editor, Michelle Rush, lost no time getting Mr. Waterford on the phone down Florida way—permission by Steve was secured.

Talking to people who know *real* adventure has a gratification with an emphasis on camaraderie that has no equal. With that association, comes the respect and good will that causes fellow Adventurers to share their worlds. Steve Waterford is an example of one of those fellow adventurers. He has produced the visual example, which typically, a sailor can only paint with the use of words. Steve's photography is in a class of its own. His ability to capture the wrath of Mother Nature is extraordinary. Please take the time to visit Steve Waterford's web page *http://www.stevewaterford.com* and The Adventurers' Club at *http://www.adventurersclub.org*

Al A. Adams

Preface

~Capt. Al A. Adams~

These 'Sea-Quences' and this book are intended for all who have fascination with the Sea. They are also for my fellow boatmen, for those whose destiny has guided them

1

away from the Sea, and for those who must make their voyages without leaving the comfort of their arm chairs.

Some of my encounters with the Sea have been harsh and dangerous, therefore, I'm pleased to share those hazards and spare you the reality—suffice that I was there.

The Sea has been kind to me, often in a rough sort of way. It has broadened, given contentment, slammed me down, and lifted me to extreme heights. The Sea is a hard taskmaster—it demands respect. If one gives the proper respect, he fares better. The Sea must be considered. It has been here a long, eventful time. A great group are lost below its surface.

Every sailing departure, every sail unfurled is because men will never get over the long romance of the past with wind, sail, and the Sea; the driving force hovers with sentiment to carry them to their adventurous goals. Sailing is wide-spread over the world and growing. It is a source of power to individuals; call it ego, call it macho, it has been a friend to man. It draws him into excitements, complacencies, hazards, and pleasures. Once he has known this life, it is difficult for him to divorce, even if he wanted to.

No matter that crafts be sleek and racy or beamy and tubby, tall rig or short and bald, they can give him pleasure and can also drive him to distraction. These vessels, whatever their types, face the same dangers of the rising Sea, the darkened sky, the sudden, 'black' or 'white' squalls, hurricanes, and pea soup fog. In these elements men face challenges to go out and return.

The simple act of sailing, for it is simple and fundamental, can bring so much to the person who indulges, is perceptive, and is aware. Preparation before departure for an extended cruise can be a world of frustrations and reversals, with a thousand problems. But casting off, severing shore ties, reduces all to the barest simplicity with only one task remaining—the achievement of the sailor's goal. One's world out there shrinks to the distance to the horizon, to the clouds, the sky, the sun, the moon, and the stars.

It is his world on board his little institution. It is his destiny and his goal. Unless one makes a departure into this world on his own sailboat, he cannot comprehend the feeling that wells within the one who makes the break. The crew cannot know that feeling—they only come close. The hardest part of a departure is the fortitude it takes to make the break and sever the ties on shore.

Epes Sargent captured the feeling well when he wrote:

> A life on the ocean wave!
> A home on the rolling deep,
> Where the scattered waters rave,
> And the winds their revels keep!

> Like an eagle caged I pine
> On this dull, unchanging shore:
> Oh give me the flashing brine,
> The spray and the tempest's roar!

There is a relationship with the vast world of the Sea that has to be earned. It takes time, much association, and much respect; those are the ingredients. When the Sea and its universe begin to show its ways, a kindred feeling manifests itself. When it happens, it is overpowering and God-like.

The Sea has secrets that are revealed to the few who go beyond the lapping restlessness, beyond the pounding surf, and beyond the ever-stretching, ever-changing horizon. To know the Sea you must not be fickle. Give of yourself, be aware, and get physically, mentally, and spiritually attuned. To know the Sea one must associate with it.

The Sea will impart its secrets and mysterious ways to those who will seek. Wade in it early; swim, bask and dive in it. Ride its waves but most important, sail its vastness in a sailboat, living the life it offers—days, months, years at a time. Pass the apprenticeship and you enter the realm of a journeyman. Become one with your boat and you will become the other with the Sea.

It is impossible to completely know the Sea from a ship. Impossible to know it from a plane in the sky, and impossible to know it from standing there on the Seashore. All of these give association, they help, they offer satisfaction, but the Sea is too grand to reveal itself so superficially.

True mountaineers know their world. Desert people, when truly in tune, know their realm. True winged birdmen of the sky feel their attunement. The earth person who passes close to the soil knows peace and understanding. Seafarers, who reach out beyond, attain a destiny and a resolution with the Sea and beyond.

Fortunate is the person who attains that great feeling in any one of those categories. But evermore blessed is the one who goes all the way, and feels that great and silent acclamation of his or her intimacy with the world.

A trend in the modern era is toward personal problems, and all the similar and attendant hang-ups that go with them. "See your shrink" seems to be the accepted solution. My solution is a boat, at Sea, as the best doctor. Your own little institution, on your own and at Sea.

Shove off, see the world in a way that only a sailboat can provide. You cannot know the world stepping out of a plane at the airport and going to the Hilton. You cannot know the world walking down a gangplank and going to a Four Seasons Resort.

The sailboat takes one where ships and planes cannot go. Then one sees and does the unexpected. People are different, usually friendlier and more exciting. Islands and places off the beaten path are unforgettable. Only a few people have sailed to more islands in the world than I.

Now, for one of the few times in my life, I have returned to a somewhat normal life style. I have begun to look upon my past as unusual, perhaps interesting. Delving deeply, I begin to feel those years of my life as proud ones. I can't help asking myself, "Has it always been this way?" Thinking back, reflecting, a good feeling courses through me. To answer my own question, "Yes, I am proud of my heritage, my way of living, my accomplishments, my years of seafaring, the challenges, the way I drove myself, the assignments I accepted with responsibility." It has been that way since time began, as it is today. It will continue so long as there are men, sailboats, and the Sea. It takes guts to seek adventure at sea.

My life has been no exception, for I feel these things strongly. On shore, even today, I strive to find a bond with land things and experiences, but none so strong, comparable and lasting has yet been found.

And so, as John Masefield said it so well:

> I must go down to the sea again,
>   to the lonely sea and the sky.
> And all I ask is a tall ship
>   and a star to steer her by.
> And the wheel's kick and the wind's
>   song and the white sails shaking,
> And a gray mist on the sea's face
>   and a gray dawn breaking.

If nothing untoward ever happened, it wouldn't be adventuresome. I like adventure.

I have tried to bring from my mind the memories of the scenes that are vivid and paint word pictures to share with you. However distinct those mental views may be, however vivid my conceptions, or however fervent my emotions, I find the phraseology at my command often is inadequate.

I often seek in vain the words I need and strive to devise forms of expression which shall portray my thoughts—and my sentiments.

A little forbearance as we put to Sea.

Adams at the navigation table with sextant, chart,
dividers, and parallel rules.

"Skipper, Are We Going to Make it?"

A Story
Depicting the Trials and Tribulations
Of a Yacht Delivery

"Vayu"

Vayu
Photo from 16mm film taken by Al A. Adams, 1946

"SKIPPER, ARE WE GOING TO MAKE IT?"

Chapter 1

Thorough Misery

One hell of a wintry dawn was about to break—one that never should have, at least not for the six of us there in the sloppy Atlantic. Seventy-five mile-an-hour spume flew in the whole northerly gale. Great masses of unwelcome water piled high over a tired and burdened ketch. Tons of water buried her as she was thrown and slued eighty feet to leeward time after time. She shuddered under this violence as sleet and hailstones driving horizontally across the wild ocean peppered her. She tried to rise to those crests of 40 foot mountains only to be slammed on her beam-ends. The whole surface of the sea was chaos of movement. The sounds were devastating. She was fighting to stay alive in the graveyard of ships off Cape Hatteras. It was winter and we were on our way to California?

I admired the *Vayu* for trying to live in these seas. For three days and nights her crew had not slept—sailing and bailing. My body shook with the cold and the seas that buried me at the helm. Solid water tried time after time to tear me from the lines that bound me. The whole gale screamed. The blasts of gale force showed they were not to be trifled with. Rain, sleet, and wind made me keep my back to windward—my face was raw, my eyes burning. Drops of spray were flung from those mountainous combers like carpet tacks. The elements tore at my oilskins and sou'wester. My rubber wool-lined Air Force boots were filled with the Atlantic—I was soaked through, cold, hungry and exhausted. It was one of those times when one finds himself in an impossible situation.

As the first light of day enlarged my world, I was thankful that now at least I could see what was ominous and not just hear the huge crashing seas. *Vayu* couldn't rise fast enough with so much weight and water thrust onto and into her.

"Skipper, Are We Going to Make it?"

Satellite View of Cape Hatteras

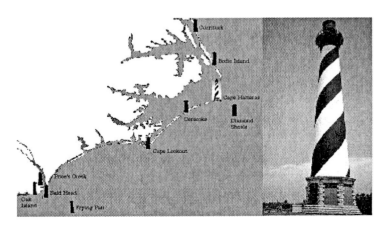

Lighthouse Map and the old Lighthouse at
Cape Hatteras originally built in 1870.

The weather didn't look good. It is said to be bad 302 days of the year off Cape Hatteras, so in preparation for anticipated heavy weather the working sails had been lowered as we departed Chesapeake Bay. I wanted to ease *Vayu* out to sea under power to give her old age consideration and lots of concern, and to let her wooden planks swell tight. The jib was unhanked and bagged; the staysail was tightly furled and gasketed with the staysail boom tightly hauled against the topping lift; the mainsail was furled, gasketed and with the sheet around the winch, her boom was hauled snug in the gallows; the mizzen was furled and gasketed. Taking departure abeam of Cape Henry into the Atlantic, we bent and reefed the heavy storm trysail. The tang of salt was heavy on the air. For further assurance, I had the fellows double sheet the storm trysail; if one sheet let go or parted, we would have a backup. The sail could take most anything, but the trimming lines (sheets) were my concern.

In the blackness of those first nights, it had been so overwhelming to suddenly be buried by solid water, terrifying to hear those breaking monsters, those vicious granddads with sheer cliff-like fronts, and not be able to see them before they engulfed us.

It was that third day, as we rose to a slab sided mass, all hell came rapping. An 87 mile-an-hour gust screamed through the rigging. The sound of the gale through her top hamper was unreal. The top eight feet of a huge wave blew off and slammed me into the spokes of the helm. This was but the forerunner, for in the next instant I was totally submerged by the great granddad, a solid comber. The roar and the power of the whole gale were wiped out, for there under solid water was my momentary respite from its roar. The lines around my waist held, but I was upside-down on the wheelbox, my head on the deck, trying to hold my breath until the gale could get to me. My nose filled with seawater and in desperation to breathe, my mouth opened too soon.

Strangling and coughing, I scrambled to get righted on the now vertical deck. The big ketch was on her port beam, flat in the solid white water in a smother of foam. She was so full of water and so inundated she wallowed to get up.

The greatest danger at sea, the most difficult to cope with, is the big wave. If we foundered under one, it would be quick. She would sink fast.

Again, a cold, green mountain of hissing, slamming water broke high over my head, as high as the mizzen mast. It curled out my starboard horizon and then wiped out my view of the deck, covering the stanchions and the davits. The boat and the sky were obliterated from my world. I was thrown by that watery tonnage hard into the spokes of the helm—breath knocked out and only water left to breathe. Strangling, I waited submerged under solid water, eyes and lungs burning from salt. I rose through it, my heart pounding, to see if the boat had survived. The terrifying crash sounded like the decks had caved in. The first sight I had was the masts and the lower spreaders lifting out of the sea at 30 degrees. Then the trying hull wallowed up slowly under tons of green water to take her place where she shouldn't be and wouldn't be if this continued. The only encouragement that I had was that she came up. She righted herself only to be buried by another, and another.

Cold and soaked through, I shook violently, un-nerved with this helpless scene. I was concerned about hypothermia; my crew below decks; their anguish, their bruises; their exhaustion from the days and nights of bailing and sailing to live. I knew someone was still hanging in there for the hose that led on deck, connected to the wobble pump under the companionway ladder, was intermittently spewing a three-quarter inch stream of pulsating bilge water over the rail to starboard. It was a manual pump so that was encouraging.

I was very concerned about Mort down in the lazarette working on the generator that had stopped at about 0300.

If kept operating, it was our chance to survive. The first day out, seas were slamming over us from both sides as we crossed the shoal area on our way to the open sea. My objective was to get free of the shallows fast and make southing because the big seas pile onto the shoals and unload their fury. They would peak, throw the boat up, and then fall out from under her. *Vayu* would drop and get buried. It was during one of these drops that the generator stopped. We had to have that generator functioning to charge the batteries that would keep the electric bilge pump going. The generator was Mort's baby and it must run or we go under.

The second morning, a sea had pitched the yacht up and slammed her hard on her port side. Sam was thrown across the main salon and hit hard on his kidney on the sharp pointed corner of the bookcase. He weighed 200 pounds and the impact was excruciating for him. The pain was too much.—he couldn't move. Frank and I carried him to his bunk. Broken ribs, a damaged kidney, vertigo, and vomiting—any one of those was too much under these conditions. While carrying him below decks, I noticed an excessive amount of bilge water sloshing over the cabin sole. Mort in the engine room also discovered that sea water was being forced into the gas tank through the vent on the outboard side of the cabin. This was a poorly installed vent the boatyard had added and was not reported in the Marine Surveyor's report before we sailed.

I was remembering the situation below decks and yet I couldn't leave the helm to get my answers. Was Mort okay? Was he in the engine room? How much water was below decks? How was Sam? He needed a doctor's help or he could die down there. The last time I attended to him was to feed him some cold broth and crackers. The stove had broken off its gimbals, so we had no hot food. I had tied Sam in his bunk forward of amidships. If he rolled into the passageway he could drown there in his cabin.

My greatest worry was for my crew below decks. The boat had taken so long to rise and right herself that with great concern I looked to see if her decks had smashed in. Maybe she had thrown some planks or the keel had dropped off. She was wallowing dangerously, and was walty and sluggish.

The main hatch slid forward and out came a body with heavy weather gear and a life harness. Out of the early light he moved aft. It was Frank shouting, "Are you okay, skipper? That last one was a bad one. The skylight gave way. Glass is below and tons of water. We've got to do something, or . . ."

"I am okay, how are the fellows?"

"They are half dead keeping the pumps going. We're in real trouble!"

An understatement from a cool crewman.

"How is Sam?"

"I am sorry, skipper. I haven't been able to get up there to his cabin. He has been crying hysterically."

"Can you take the helm?"

"Yes."

"Who is on the wobble pump?"

"Dick. He is vomiting dry heaves now, but he keeps that pump going."

"Where is the owner?"

"I haven't seen the bastard since midnight. I don't want to see him. I might kill him. He refuses to help us bail. He kept saying, 'This is the finest yacht in the world.' He acts funny."

This yelling dialogue went on as I ran *Vayu* off before the next sea to allow Frank to get his safety lines well secured. The skylight was another problem that needed immediate attention. Frank was hollow-eyed and pale as he tied himself to the wheelbox. I quickly oriented him and gave him our course SW by W a 1/4W. He repeated the course and said, "Shit, this is a goddam screamer!"

"We have no choice now," I said. "This course will take us into the beach. Keep her up as much as you can. If we miss Charleston, we'll go for the beach. She is sinking too fast. I'd like to sail her faster but she leaks too much when I press her. She has all the sail up she can use. This is a devastatingly slow race for survival."

Frank saw the next sea coming and grabbed me as the huge growler buried us. Wrenched from his grasp, I washed down the tops of the stanchions and lifelines, and came up sharp, feet first, against the heavy teak chocks of the launch amidships. God was with me. Had I gone on the outboard side of the lifelines, I would have been buried at sea off Cape Hatteras and missed a hell of a lifetime of good sailing.

Frank looked relieved as I scrambled aft under difficulty. Fighting the gale for admittance to the hatch, I ducked below. The next hissing mountain of green slammed *Vayu* over on her side as I forced the hatch closed.

The sight below was a real depressing chiller. In the past six and a half hours I could only imagine the scene below decks. Now came the impact of our predicament. In short, we were sinking 250 miles offshore. *Vayu* was 76 feet long, mahogany planked with teak decks, and was beautifully designed. She was built by Nathaniel G. Herreshoff in 1899, fine lined and fast. She carried a press of working sail that had to be reckoned with, for in this gale and pounding she would have driven under and floundered days ago had we carried more sail than the trysail and storm jib she was now carrying. I was under pressure. Six lives and a fine, old, tired yacht were looking to me for survival. I was looking to God and a tired, old yacht.

Below, a sight was revealed that no boatman should have to see—especially when he is exhausted, cold, hungry and debilitated. I hesitated a moment on the top rung of the companionway ladder as a big sea piled over the deck.

Solid water came shooting through the skylight. Under the ladder I saw Dick standing in water to his knees. Water in the main salon was splashing over the table legs. As the tired, old yacht rolled, the water surged up and hit the overhead. Unbelievable!! The surging, sloshing water floated charts, oranges, apples, sleeping bags, bread, pencils, cookies in cellophane, pamphlets, wrappers, boxes of film, clothes, shoes, boots with their soles up, oil skins, the salt shaker, rolls of toilet paper, and the corker was a half empty bottle of Scotch. Imagine it and it was there! No wonder she was wallowing! Dick was vomiting, his head in the crook of one arm, while the other arm kept the wobble-type pump going. He was trying—doing more than his part—green as he was; most people are helpless when seasick.

I slid into the mess, spoke to Dick and made my way aft to the engine room. As I went by I could see water dripping out of the ship-to-shore radio. That took care of that! No radio aid.

A big, full sail bag had jammed against the engine room door. Mort was in there. I frantically pulled the bag away and opened the door as heavy gasoline odor hit me. I yelled, "Mort, are you okay?" There he was in that foul air, vomit was everywhere and with it the heavy gasoline odor was sickening. He answered, "Okay." I knew he wasn't but that was Mort. He was unbeatable. Gasoline, bilge water, vomit, and stale air—what a romantic way to go to sea! Mort was an awful green color, but still he worked. As he explained, it became obvious why the generator had stopped. Seawater entering the vent was going into the gas tank and on into the carburetor. I couldn't believe that, in these violent rolls and in this sickening atmosphere, Mort had taken the carburetor apart, removed the water, cleaned the parts, and reassembled them. He was now under the tank draining gasoline and sea water into a shallow little stew pan, which was all that would fit under the tank. He was separating the liquids and was filling a quart-sized can which would now become the improvised gas tank for the vital generator. This can was wedged in so, hopefully, it wouldn't fall as the boat rolled. The main engine was quarter submerged with seawater. Fortunately, the batteries were high enough not to be submerged.

Mort was trying to vomit as he indicated he was ready to try starting the generator. It was a dry heave. I told him not to try to start the generator until I opened the hatch over his head. If he hit the starter with all that raw gas and heavy fumes, we would blow her planks off. He said, "Thanks, good thought." He needed air. He had been breathing the heavy fumes so long he was impervious to them.

I aired the engine room and lazarette between the seas pouring in, and then gave him the okay. What a relief and what music that was as the generator started. Good old Mort. I helped him put on his oil skins over the vomit, and with his sou'wester and boots retrieved, I got him into the dog house for air and seawater. He needed sleep badly. There below decks I walked with my hands as well as my feet. As she rolled dangerously, I was aware of a new creaking sound I hadn't heard while topside. She was working badly. Those sounds were disturbing. She was too tired for this violence. In spite of her condition, she still had an irrepressible air of ability to do battle with gale force winds. Her days of magnificent sailing, it appeared, were numbered; maybe ours, too.

Next, and very imperative, I found the lengths of wood I had cut to size at the boatyard in case of emergency. They were the same dimensions as the yacht's planks in case we stove a hole in her if we should run into a heavy object. I found a big sail bag, the hammer and some boat nails. It was miserable spending so much energy working my way through the boat. Once, as water poured over me from where the deck skylight had been, I found, as she wallowed over on her beam, that I was walking on the glass of the ports.

Crew from *VAYU* before the storm hit. (l. to r.)
Dick, Al, Sam, Frank and Mort
Photo from collection of Al Adams

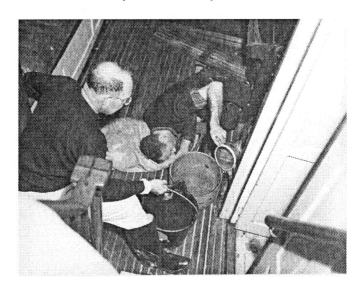

Bailing on the *VAYU*.
Photo from collection of Al Adams

That slow, uneasy wallowing roll—if she rolled over with all this water inside she would sink before she could right herself. Her center of effort was wrong with all this water below decks. Those awful mushy moments . . . we had her battened down but with the big skylight broken out she would sink fast. I was worried about the fellows below— they wouldn't have a chance, but then none of us would. The small row boat wouldn't survive in these seas. It couldn't stay afloat in this maelstrom if we had to take to it. Conditions that were overwhelming to a yacht of this size would give little chance to our skiff.

I hurried to the deck, secured my safety line to a pad eye in the deck adjacent to the skylight, and quickly threw the sail bag over the demolished skylight. The planks were then placed tight to the sides of the missing skylight over the four edges of the sail bag and nailed in place onto the teak deck. That job done, I hurried below to try to encourage Dick, then forward through the oily mess to Sam's cabin. As I forced the door open against all that water, there was Sam crying for his wife and daughter. He looked awful. His face was badly swollen. He looked up as the bilge water surged over him, as he lay lashed in the bunk.

"Skipper, are we going to make it?"

It was a hell of a good question. There weren't too many plusses in our favor. If only we had another person to help— that bastard of an owner lying drunk in his cabin. But that was wishful thinking; he wasn't even any help to himself.

"Hell, yes, Sam. Hang on. We'll make it!!"

It was obvious that Sam's kidney was injured, for uremic poisoning was causing him to swell. He had to have liquids to help flush his system. I dug out a bottle of distilled water and told him to force down all the water he could. I gave him two codeine tablets, and a tin of dry sea biscuits to munch on and to help curb his seasickness. It was a sloppy, smelly hellhole for Sam.

The generator was music—it meant the pump was operating. Dick was exhausted. I spelled him on the wobble pump while he got some air. It was dismal under the companionway ladder as I pumped.

The gale diminished in the afternoon to a steady 60 miles per hour. We had to organize our strength and thinking.

Chapter 2

"The Finest Yacht In The World" . . . ?

How did this all happen? Why were we out here? The following is what took place in California.

The phone rang that late summer day in Los Angeles. The year was 1945. It was an attorney friend who enjoyed sailing his power boat to Catalina Island. We had attended the Los Angeles Yacht Club Wednesday luncheon the week before at the Los Angeles Athletic Club.

"Al, how are you? A friend of mine who once owned a powerboat has purchased a beautiful 76' ketch. It is on Chesapeake Bay. He doesn't sail. I have told him about you. He wants to sail the yacht to California by way of the Panama Canal. Will you skipper her around? If you like, he will take us to lunch tomorrow to get acquainted. Can you meet me at my office?"

"Yes. How is 12 noon?"

"Great. See you then."

The new owner was a big, powerful man, large and overly friendly. We lunched at Little Joe's downtown. He brought drawings of the yacht. The vessel impressed me as I scanned her hull drawings and sail plan.

"What do you think of her?" he asked, over his martini. "Her name is *Vayu*[1]."

---

[1]   Vayu—In Hinduism, Vayu is a wind god.

"She was well conceived, looks fast. My concern is her age. Did you have a good, close Marine Survey done when she was purchased?"

"Yes, she passed a fine survey. Here is a copy."

I looked it over while they chatted. The survey—very wordy—was a lengthy description of where the owner's cabin was located, spacious galley, 15 bags of sails, but nothing said about their condition. Engine reportedly rebuilt, but no indication what year. Sleeps 10. Rigging okay as viewed from the deck. The recommendations were to paint the bottom, put water in the batteries and stitch the mains'l cover.

My glancing up from the report clued him in and we began boat talk. "Mr. Adams, what do you think of her now?"

"Well, sir, I have many questions. I trust you will not mind. I don't mean to be discourteous."

"Not at all. I am pleased to hear what you will say."

"First, this survey doesn't tell me what I would like to know were I buying this craft. For her age, I would want to know about her planks, her frames and her fastenings. I would want to see three samples of her fastenings in my hands. One sample from 12 inches above her water line, one at the water line and one five inches below the water line. I would want to know if her keel bolts were going to hold that big lead keel on. Are they wasted with all these years of potential corrosion? How good is her wiring? Is it salted? How good are her sea cocks and sea valves and her through-hull fittings? What is the condition of the rudder and rudder hangers? I would suggest the rudder be lowered to inspect the condition of the rudderpost, the blade, and the internal steering assembly. I don't like for a surveyor to tell me the rigging is okay as seen from the deck. That means nothing. Is there any bad wood in the masts and spreaders? What is the condition of her tangs and sheaves? In all these years, the odds are that there is bad wood some place in the vessel. Am I being too critical? We must think of these things before she goes to sea. It is a long stretch of ocean to California. You indicate you want me to assemble a crew and to skipper her around to the West Coast. Will you be on board? My first concern is the safety of all on board and, secondly, your investment. Thank you for hearing me out."

"You impress me, Mr. Adams." He scanned the survey. "I see what you mean. You see, the broker told me this is the finest yacht in the world. Yes, I will be on board."

"I question how a surveyor who probably doesn't know how to sail—judging from his nomenclature and written recommendations, and who has possibly never really been to sea and doesn't seem to own a gantline and bos'n's chair—can give a good report? It may be the finest yacht ever, but right now, I question that report and the broker."

"Where are we then and what should be done?"

"I would have another Marine Surveyor from perhaps Boston or Baltimore go down there and make a haul-out survey. As you are anxious to get started, I will assemble a crew right away, but we don't go east until the survey indicates she is healthy . . . with no blatant recommendations or problems."

"Agreed. I'll call you," he said quickly.

"Thanks for the lunch, gentlemen." I was away.

Two days later the owner called to say he had located another surveyor. He had called the yard manager to have him haul the yacht. The survey would be forthcoming.

"That is good progress. I have a crew all set. A fine group, with good sailing experience."

"Great," he said, "I'll call you when the report arrives. We will have a dinner at my home and get acquainted. I forgot to tell you, the boatyard is building a fine teak doghouse over the cockpit. They are also installing a big bank of heavy-duty submarine batteries aft in the engine room, a four-cylinder gasoline generator, and a tank aft for 100 gallons more gasoline."

I gulped and there was my long silence. To myself I said, 'How could a good boatyard do this to an unsuspecting new boat owner? Just to keep the yard going in the fall and winter months, they are ruining a fine, old racing boat suggesting these unnecessary, expensive additions to one who would fall for it. That is scandalous. *Vayu* is not a heavy cruising boat. She is a fast, old hull that shouldn't have that added weight.'

From the phone, "Mr. Adams, are you there?"

"Oh, yes. Yes, sir, I am sorry. I was mentally back on the yacht at the boatyard. Let's wait now for the survey."

"Okay," he said, "I'll call you just as soon as it arrives. Good day."

Several days later the phone call came from the owner. The survey I had asked for, after all the boatyard additions and work orders had been completed, had arrived. He read the new survey report to me over the phone.

"Great report," he said, "clean bill of health." He was now anxious to get my opinion, meet the crew, and get the show on the road. Could we all meet for dinner at his home, say six o'clock Friday? I called all the fellows—they were ready. Dick, Mort, Frank, Sam, and I arrived. By way of introductions of a great crew: Dick had sailed on many racing yachts, had crewed with me, and crewed on the famous schooner, *Morning Star* when she set the elapsed time record of 10:10:13:09.5 in the 1949 Transpacific Race to Honolulu. He had participated in five Transpacific Races to Honolulu, Hawaii. Mort shook hands with the owner. Mort and Dick had sailed together. Mort had owned several fine boats and knew his way around the ocean. Frank was just out of the service and in good physical condition. He had crewed with me many miles at sea and had sailed on the 104' schooner *Dwyn Wen* in the offshore submarine patrol service during World War II. Sam was the outgoing, life of a good crew, a hard worker. He and Frank would bleed on the boat if I asked. Sam had sailed with me on many boats I had skippered, from 21 feet up to the 136' schooner *Enchantress*.

Morning Star
Photo from Dick Brownell collection.

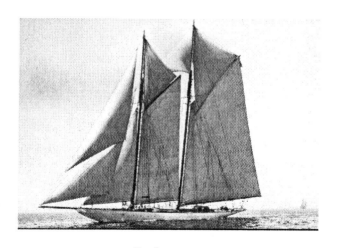

Enchantress
Photo from Al Adams collection. Original taken by W.C. Sawyer
Courtesy of Newport Harbor Nautical Museum

He sailed on the old *Lanakai* out of Honolulu when it went on the search for the Dole flyers lost at sea years before. He sailed out to Hermes Reef and Midway Island on that search. The lost flyers were racing from Oakland, California to Honolulu, Hawaii in 1927 and were never found.

They were a great crew to live with and wore well at sea, which to me are great attributes. The ability to live with people at sea under difficult conditions is very important and is vital to a successful voyage. Sailing ability can be learned but compatibility must be brought on board.

We had a fine crew of low-key individuals. The owner voiced his approval, announced that Mr. Adams would be the skipper, and that he would be the navigator. A round of drinks were served. The owner handed me the new survey to read. A gut feeling hit me with these surveys. "Sir, these reports are too good. Will you get another surveyor? Too much is at stake."

He wanted to blow up but saw that I didn't care if he did.

"Okay," he said, "I'll get another out of Boston."

I was relieved.

While I continued going over the survey, the maid was preparing a very fine dinner. The owner asked if anyone would like another drink. For the most part, the fellows were not heavy drinkers. One cocktail seemed to be all that any of us cared for. The owner at that time made what I thought was a very good suggestion and, to me, indicated that he was serious in this endeavor. He said there would be one rule on the boat to which he would like to definitely adhere. There would be no drinking while under way. All agreed to this wholeheartedly. I was glad that he had made this suggestion because it is one of the rules I have always kept while under way. Alcohol and sailing do not mix. The owner again indicated that he would be the navigator. It was his boat and we would be glad to have him navigate. At that, he brought out his navigational equipment.

Dwyn Wen aka: "Dirty D"
Photo from Al Adams Collection. Original taken by W. C. Sawyer
Courtesy of Newport Harbor Nautical Museum.

It was immediately noticeable to me that he had been to the war surplus store to pick up his bearing taker, taffrail log, and sextant (a bubble sextant used by the Air Force navigators and one which should be modified to make it useable on a surface vessel). He brought out his charts, dividers, parallel rules, and bits of gear that are recommended and necessary for the type of navigating we would be doing. I became concerned, though, when I asked him, "Have you pumped out the bubble in the bubble sextant?" He had never heard of this before and it was then that I was beginning to question his navigating ability. A bubble sextant is almost impossible to use on a rolling boat. Some of the other pieces of surplus equipment could be used on large vessels at sea and some could be used on aircraft. Some of it would be useable on a small craft at sea. He brought out some charts, which were not completely adequate in that they did not make a complete chain of coverage from the Chesapeake to the Panama Canal and up the Pacific Coast to California. I wanted to make sure he had the Sailing Directions for the Atlantic and Pacific Coasts. These he said he would pick up. Things were not looking just exactly right. I thought, 'Well, this picture will go together.' We were called to the table for a very pleasant dinner in fine surroundings. It was a jovial evening. The crew and owner were getting acquainted as we discussed all of the usual and necessary items for such a voyage. It was decided that each would bring heavy weather gear, sleeping bag, boots, etc. The owner asked us if we could depart in four days and each indicated that he could. He would then get tickets for the train.

I received the third survey on the ketch, and as I perused it, I still couldn't imagine that a boat built in 1899 could have such a clear record. There were no major recommendations. Practically all items mentioned were unimportant. It was hard for me to refute anything that was said because three prominent surveyors had now given the boat a clean bill of health and that's what we were looking for.

As agreed, we arrived at the depot to depart for Washington, D.C. The owner arrived late—and drunk!

We had quite a lot of gear on the train, all necessary for a cruise to California. From Washington, D.C., we took a cab down to the boat on Chesapeake Bay. As we drove up to the boatyard, we looked anxiously at the big ketch tied at the dock waiting for us. The owner's first question to me was, "There she is; how do you like her?"

At that first moment, I was registering deep concern. Looking at the boat, as she was lying there with her starboard side to me, it was obvious that all of the extra equipment and additions made by the boatyard were detrimental to the welfare of the boat. She was sitting so deep in the water that her counter was under water. Forward that beautiful bow was sticking up 24" above her waterline. This was what had concerned me when I read the work orders from the boatyard while in Los Angeles, and now there it was. It was obvious. So to answer his question I said, "She's a great vessel if you take all of that heavy equipment out of her."

This was very upsetting to the owner and his next question was, "Well, what can we do about it? It's done now and it has cost me a lot of money."

"The boat would be better off and will be more apt to survive if all that heavy equipment is removed."

"What is the effect of this?" he asked.

"The boat is sitting in the water so poorly trimmed, her bow is going to lift and with every big sea she'll take a beating. Her potential boat speed is sadly defeated. She will be dragging her counter through the water, which will kill her speed by at least two knots. The thing I am concerned about is whether she will survive in a real heavy sea condition. Did you notice the last surveyor didn't even mention this?"

The owner asked, "What can I do?"

I thought for a while and said, "What can be done, should not be done. It would take a ton of weight forward to get her bow down. To do so would defeat the boat because she is not built for that excess weight in her ends. She would suffer because of the attempt to get her back level in the water. I wouldn't add weight to her because it will defeat such an old boat."

It was then that we should have aborted the trip. If we could have sailed by way of the inland waterway from the Chesapeake down inside Cape Hatteras to Beaufort, North Carolina, or on down to Florida and then gone out to sea, perhaps we could have aided this vessel in her attempt to reach California. But this was impossible because the inland waterway was dredged to ten feet and the way the big ketch was riding, she must draw twelve feet. With the weight of the crew and their gear we would add another 1,000 pounds to the yacht. This would add to her problem of seaworthiness and defeat the trip because she would immediately run aground in the inland waterway, exceeding the dredged depth of 10 feet. I explained the problem to the fellows and asked for a vote. "Do we go home or sail her around Cape Hatteras?" They voted to sail and move out of this cold. So that's where we were. We walked down to the boat and stowed our gear below then walked around and looked the vessel over below decks and topsides. She was impressive.

From sunny California to the bitter cold Chesapeake in the wintertime was quite a change to us. We moved on board, each took a cabin and tried to get comfortable. Ice was forming around the boat. It snowed every night. It was miserable to have blizzards, sweep snow each day, and try to get work done on the boat to get ready to sail to California. On board in the main salon was a little oil heater which we fired up, keeping it livable amidships, but in the quarters where our bunks were, it was impossible to get warm.

The water in this part of the bay was brackish and freezing. The ice forming outside had crept closer to the boat each day and the ice at the waterline was directly in contact with the planks adjacent to our foam rubber mattresses. The cold penetrated through the hull and into the rubber mattresses, and we missed a lot of sleep because it was impossible to get warm. We tried to bundle up in the main salon and see it through until the boat was ready. We were miserably cold. Several days were spent provisioning, fueling up, checking out the boat, checking the engine, and breaking out the sails to check their condition. It was interesting, as we raised the mains'l, to watch chunks of ice fall on the deck from the folds where water had collected.

It was necessary to quickly get acquainted with the boat. I went aloft in the bos'n chair and inspected the tangs and rigging, replaced some blocks, and rove new halyards. The running rigging was too old to go to sea.

It was time to take the boat on an initial sail to see if everything was functioning. We departed from the dock and went out into the bay. It was blowing 25 m.p.h. We made sail and tacked around the bay. Frank was at the helm as we were coming back up to the channel heading back toward the boatyard. He was pinching her close hauled trying to get around a buoy but got headed and lost way. The boat fell away and went about five feet from the marker, and was into the mud. It was cold and miserable just being out there sailing but to be aground was something else. Frank was all apologetic but it really wasn't his fault. It was just that the boat was headed and she lost steerage at a crucial moment. We went on the mud at such a slow speed that I felt with various tactics we could get her off. We flattened the mains'l, backed the jib, and tried to get her to spin on her forefoot by carrying all the crew's weight on the foredeck. She wanted to move but wasn't quite doing it, so we walked all the crew back and forth amidships at the position of the mainmast, and rolled her back and forth so she would dig a trench with her keel and hopefully move out. All of these tactics just about worked, but not quite. I had the fellows put the small row boat in the water and take a big kedge anchor out on her port quarter aft into the channel. With this anchor out about 300 feet from the boat and the hawser secured to one of the big genoa winches, we started hauling on the line. With flattened sails and all of us using our weight as best we could in an attempt to make her roll, she finally answered and swung out toward the big kedge. Once out of the mud, we dropped the sails quickly and started the engine, which I had used only for a moment while in the mud, and then cut it off not wanting the mud to get sucked into the water intake. That would have worn out the water pump impellers of the engine cooling system. While still at anchor with the sails dropped and furled, I decided to go aloft and take a look at the water between the next channel marker and us. It was well that I did because, with her very deep keel and low tide, we would have run aground again even though we were in the proper channel. It was a good exercise with no harm done. We made our way back to the dock and secured. I didn't like the way she sailed with her bow so high out of the water and dragging her counter but we decided to make the best of it.

The next day I took a truck provided by the boatyard and went into the village to get our perishable provisions and other last minute items that were on our checklist. While I was in shopping, our boat owner had gone to the yard office and ordered a ton of lead pigs, which were stowed forward by the time I returned late that afternoon. They were stowed forward of her point of immersion to get her bow down. I was sorry to see this happen and I told the owner that it was not the smart thing to do, and would probably be her undoing if we got into heavy weather. He assumed that it would be okay because the yard manager had said it would be fine.

Departure time was near. The manager of the boatyard was getting a bit nervous and came to the boat with the horrendous bill. The owner paid the bill over a round of Scotch. The manager then asked if we would move the yacht to another location because he had another vessel coming in.

Adams, Commodore of Cabrillo Beach Yacht Club,
raising CBYC's burgee over the *Vayu*.
Photo from Al Adams collection

We moved between some upright pilings for the rest of the day and night. Lying there we found we were in good company, for next to us was the *When And If*, General George Patton's yacht. It was under a full fitted canvas cover and covered with snow. Icicles hung from the bottom perimeter of the cover. I was impressed with the name of his boat. It told a sad story. Both waiting for the other, the long wait— the sad ending with the General's demise.

I hated the thought of going out to sea around Cape Hatteras under the boat's condition. However, early the next morning, we made our departure from the dock and moved out into the Chesapeake ready for our departure around Cape Henry. Another vote—a cold crew voted, "Let's go!" We put to sea. It was bitter cold but clear. The weather indicated a low-pressure cell offshore and very unsettled weather, but we were anxious to get out to sea into the Gulf Stream and be down abeam of Florida and warming up. Our initial course was to take us well offshore to clear Cape Hatteras in case of bad weather.

We discussed and set the course to move offshore, and at the same time get some southing. The wind was fresh out of the North and bitter cold, giving us a very broad reach, almost a run on this course. The swells were big and white-capped. The fellows were busy on deck getting her secure for sea. They seemed happy among themselves but it was obvious hate was brewing for the owner who had shown his bad temper when drunk. He wouldn't help with the gear and boat handling because he knew nothing about sailing. The unimportant incident of getting stuck in the bay mud was being referred to with his razor's edge of vehemence. Had he been at the helm in the bay instead of Frank it would very likely have happened to him.

In an attempt to relieve this tension, I asked the owner-navigator if he had made departure entries in the logbook and would he give me our initial course? He left the deck. We were rolling and pitching in the cold norther. Forty minutes went by and he didn't come up to give a course nor did he make entries in the logbook. Mort took the helm while I plotted our course on the chart and determined the distance to travel before changing course. I had previously streamed the log to run the distance between channel markers to calibrate for accuracy. Entries in the log were made assuming the owner was seasick since he didn't come on deck.

The sea was empty except for a gaggle of noisy sea birds making a sharp, shrill squabble over a school of fish being maneuvered by a brace of sharks and fish below them.

I anticipated making a dogleg course change later about 80 miles at sea and then head on down toward the Windward Passage in the Bahamas making our initial stop at Watling

Island, San Salvador, the island where Columbus landed when he discovered the West Indies and the New World.

I thought it was odd that the owner kept his cabin locked all the time at the dock and now at sea, and as three o'clock in the afternoon approached, I was beginning to get the answer. We were well offshore. The owner seemed to be setting a pattern—at the dock at three o'clock in the afternoon he was locked in his cabin. Now at sea for the first time, he was in his cabin and when he came out we got the answer. It was his decision in California that there would be no drinking while under way. He was the first to break that rule coming out of his cabin at about four thirty, extremely drunk, extremely belligerent. In an attempt to show his macho image, he grabbed Frank and bodily lifted him and shoved him against the overhead to show how powerful he was. This didn't go over very big with Frank who looked to me for a decision as to how to accept this attack. Aside, I told him to take it easy and let's get *Vayu* on down into warm weather. It was miserable sailing and it was beginning to get more miserable living with an alcoholic owner, a Jekyll and Hyde: overly friendly when sober, three drinks and then overly belligerent. When he was drunk, he felt extremely strong, was very argumentative and very difficult to live with. He usually passed out in his cabin after locking the door behind him. We were very happy to have him go to his cabin. He was a menace on deck and hard to live with.

That Frank had come to hate him was obvious. Each day the dislike for him grew and spread to the others. I later learned the owner had eight cases of Scotch in his cabin. That was to be a lot of headaches for him and indirectly for the crew.

Chapter 3

A Furious World

A gale force was building and blew with spite. It blew without interval and without mercy. Our world out here was under a sky that hovered menacingly above *Vayu's* masts—a world out of which great, foaming waves rushed at us. In this watery, stormy space there was as much flying spray as there was air. There was the constant howling of the wind, the tumult of the sea, the crash of water slamming over the decks. It was a most formidable storm. I felt sorry for the old, tired ketch. There was no rest for her—no rest for us. It was as if we were bewitched within the circle of the sea horizon. *Vayu* pitched and rolled violently; incessantly she stood on her bow, sat on her stern, rolled, and groaned. Our every move on board under this beating was with constant effort and worry. The routine of watches was no more, for we couldn't spare anyone under these conditions. The faces of the crew, when I could glimpse them, were weary and serious. I felt as though the only things on our side were youth—and God. We were committed in this fury. We couldn't turn back yet maybe we couldn't go on. It was grimly looking that way. Had *Vayu* been healthy, this sail would have been a fun challenge. Now she was working herself loose, leaking badly—not yet enough to drown us at once but enough to kill us at the pumps. It was depressing to look at the seas rolling high as far as the eye could reach, their tops white with foam and their bodies a deep indigo streaked with gale friction. Hour after hour they came without respite, seas crashing and thundering over us.

It was a furious world—no sky, no stars—nothing but high wind, angry clouds and infuriated seas. The thought of warm, wholesome food, well-prepared, was maddening and tantalizing.

My youth was being tested—the feeling that I could last forever was waning. There was a numbness of spirit. The long stress of the gale had done it. The suspense of the interminably culminating catastrophe saddens—body fatigue results in the mere holding on to existence within this excessive tumult. Would we outlast the sea? Would we see another sunrise?

Before us was a big ocean, tossing now with cross-seas bringing the turbulence of another not-too-distant storm which could continue to make this passage a nightmare. The sky was threatening, as was the sea—not too many things in our favor in this scene.

Vayu was leaking badly. We couldn't turn back against the building northerly gale for when we pressed her, water came in faster than we could bail. All I could do was reduce sail and creep toward shore by broad reaching toward Charleston, South Carolina, or the beach. I couldn't head for the Bahamas—they were too far and to find a boatyard there that could haul her out for repairs was impossible. She would sink. Heading in toward shore, it appeared, was our only chance to survive. I must sail her only as fast as we could keep up with the water coming into her. Sam needed a doctor fast. The owner wouldn't help us bail and was useless at the helm. Animosity was growing.

Frank reported to me after another session with the owner, "Skipper, you have plenty to think about, but I just want to say, in the Navy I was taught to kill. You say the word and either that bastard or I will go over the rail—and it won't be me."

Frank was very loyal. I knew his hostility for the owner was getting too serious but I felt he would come to me before he would tackle a problem of this magnitude—getting rid of the source of his hate.

The dawn's light came up beneath this threatening dome of gale and torn clouds. From horizon to horizon there pushed closer and closer great lurching masses of froth and solid water, everything that moved out there seemed to endanger us—an ill-omened seascape.

We bailed and sailed and hungered for hot food. But that was not to be—the stove wouldn't work. Optimistically opening cans, whose labels were reposing in bilge water, we had a 99 percent average—mixed fruit salad. Not once a day but four times a day. For three days our average remained. We didn't bail well on gallon tins of fruit salad. Dick was going to break our average—he opened three more gallon cans—all fruit salad. More tries. We got lucky! A can of green olives and a can of sauerkraut. Not bad with fruit salad and seawater. We hunched down in the cold, wet doghouse and passed the cans to each other between the breaking seas.

At noon Mort sighted a ship on the horizon. By its course, we determined she might be coming up from Panama, and if we came about we could close reach and converge with her. Adrenalin flowed as we picked a trough between the big seas and jibed. I hated to sail her close hauled into this stuff because the water came into her all the faster. She was working badly, creaking and groaning all the more.

The ship turned out to be an oil tanker. On she came with a bone in her teeth, slamming into the gale. She buried her bow and scooped the seas over her catwalk amidships all the way back to the bridge.

I yelled, "Run up the colors upside down. Get the owner's gun, the flare gun, and everyone wave your arms. Get their attention!"

U.S. Flag upside down indicating vessel in distress.
Photo by Al Adams, Skipper

We raced to converge with the ship heading North against the seas. We were slamming and burying, filling with water and getting more and more sluggish. We were converging with our port bow to their starboard side forward of their beam. The American flag was flying upside down from our starboard spreader, an obvious SOS signal to be respected at sea. Frank fired the .38 into the sky and Mort fired the Very pistol sending up a parachute flare. All of us were waving our arms or clothes and spontaneously yelling, which, of course, couldn't be heard in this gale.

The ship was now about 350 feet from us, her bow buried one moment and propeller revolving free of the water the next, then the blades slapped the water as she buried her stern and shoved her bow high to slam back into the trough.

The tanker was deep down on its Plimsol Marks, heavily laden with oil or gasoline. As close as we were, when we dropped over a big wave and down into the trough we could not see the ship. Rising on the next wave was like looking out from an inspiration point for there she was, full length, so close—and not a person in sight.

We yelled, fired the Very pistol again, waved our oil skins—everyone on deck prayed we would be seen. We had sailed back into that pounding sea for three miles to converge with that ship and now it sailed on. No one on her decks. She didn't slow. It was so vital to us, that contact with help was so all-important. Now she was moving away into those burying seas. We were torn between hope and anger.

I took the .38 from Frank and aimed it at the stern of that ship—for one awful moment—then lowered the gun as tears rolled into the salt crystals on my face.

Bearing away, I changed course to have the yacht's full beam exposed to the departing ship in case someone just might be looking aft. To no avail—the ship disappeared over the violent horizon.

We were dejected, crushed, exhausted. *Vayu* was really full of seawater now. I said, "Fellows, we must think solely of survival. We are not defeated. Let's all turn to and bail before she sinks. Pumps, bucket brigade—let's give it our best. Let's bail!! The dinghy won't survive in these seas so let's try to keep the yacht afloat as long as we can."

We were calling upon strength we felt impossible to muster.

Chapter 4

So This Is Yachting

We dropped the storm trysail and let *Vayu* lie ahull to ride to the seas. We formed a bucket brigade and in three hours we had the water down to where the cabin sole was awash. The boat was working, but I didn't realize just how much until I looked down at the base of the main bulkhead in the salon. It was lifting free of the sole and moving back down with each sea. We were in deep trouble, very deep! I didn't know how long she could take this strain before she might break up—or break down to Davy Jones' Locker.

With the volume of water reduced we got Sam up in the doghouse and tied him down. We encouraged him to drink a lot of water and gave him another codeine tablet. He was suffering with every roll of the vessel but it was better to get him out of that hellhole and vomit stench. The air was better topside and the seawater was fresher but just as wet. Hunger pains persisted and so did our average—three cans of fruit salad before we found one of cold pork and beans. Would I ever like fruit salad again?

As night came on we raised the trysail. The gale was building again and once more water was eight inches over the cabin sole. We bailed, traded off at the helm, and each man of the three slept one hour. Mort climbed back in the engine compartment every hour and drained off some more gasoline, separated the salt water from it,

45

Vayu crew "enjoying" more fruit cocktail.

and kept the generator going. That power-driven bilge pump, going full-time, wasn't keeping up with the water coming in. However, with the wobble pump and bucket brigade, she might make the beach before our strength was spent—if she didn't throw her planks.

The charts were soaked. My dead-reckoning position was approximately 90 miles offshore and about 115 miles from Charleston. Could we make it? Every night, and in the daytime as well, if we sighted a ship on the horizon, we fired the Very pistol sending up parachute flares. No avail. Surely, they couldn't all be on auto-pilot as their crews slept.

To have one man off watch for each hour to rest was a problem. With Sam totally incapacitated and unavailable to help bail or to take the helm, and the owner, on alcohol, not willing to accept the fact we were in trouble, the remaining three of us bore the burden.

Just before noon on the fourth day, the wind eased to 55 m.p.h. The seas were high. The speed of the boat had to be kept under four knots and the course was as easy as we could give her, broad reaching for the closest land. If we tried to sail fast, we couldn't keep up with the intake of water from so many places. We could hear the water coming in, but analyzing her structure internally, we would have to chop into her ceiling and cabinetry to get to it. We couldn't waste our energy on those endeavors, for the areas that leaked were too many and too great. By her working, she must be chewing out the caulking between her planks. My decisions were bail and sail and pray. We did all three. We would sink if our routine was interrupted. Collision mats or blankets pulled tight against her planks externally (under water) or sails pulled hard against the planks with lines tied to their clews, peaks and tacks would possibly work, but would take time and energy we didn't have. While doing these sensible chores, we could sink. We faced a dilemma and had to do the right thing, so when the water got up to slosh on the bunks in the main salon, we three had to go to the buckets.

In late afternoon, we rolled along under reefed trysail. I was at the helm. Sam was in the doghouse sobbing with pain. Frank, Mort, and Dick came up from bailing looking gaunt and hollow-eyed—still in their oilskins and boots. Actually, we hadn't taken off these heavy weather clothes and long underwear since arriving at the boatyard nearly 10 days ago. We were pungent so kept to weather of each other—almost!

The storm trysail sheet was doubled making two parts from the clew to the fairleads at the rail. The boat was rolling hard to the leftover seas from the gale. The wind was now blowing at 30 m.p.h. and the trysail was trimmed flat as a board to slow the boat's speed. Our speed was still about 4 knots. It would have been so nice to let her sail but we couldn't. She would have sailed to Davy Jones' Locker.

The crew was gathered at the helm to discuss our plight. All were in life jackets and safety harnesses. The main hatch slid open and out came our 235-lb. alcoholic owner, well heeled and belligerent. He stepped out on deck just as the boat rolled her lee rail deep under. He was caught off balance and went flying head long over the rail. His body was completely beyond the lifelines over the water. Save for the fact that the trysail sheet was doubled, he would have been thrown into those rough seas. Clad in all those heavy clothes, oilskins, and boots, I doubt if he would have been able to stay up. Being drunk was also not in his favor. The yacht would have been slow to answer the helm and difficult to maneuver back to him with reduced sail, rough seas, and no engine.

His head went directly between those two taut lines, the sheets to the trysail. They hit hard on his shoulders and precisely on time the yacht rolled back to weather. Like a giant bow and strings, they threw him back, belly down, over the lifeline, as the sea came up on him and washed his sou'wester hat off his balding head. His fluffy red hair, now soaked and darkened, was like unruly skeins of oakum streaked around his bare red skull. His face, glistening with seawater, was crimson. He was mad, scared, and drunk—a hell of a combination.

It was at this point that I felt the full impact of the hate that existed, for not one of us there on deck made a move to help. He climbed back badly shaken, no doubt bruised. Not one word was spoken. He crawled the deck on all fours to the hatch and went below.

When he was out of earshot, I called the fellows to me. "Look, fellows, I was part of that scene, just as you were. Do you realize that not one of us made a move to help him? This has to stop! I realize how we all feel toward the bastard but let's be considerate, at all costs."

They agreed. The weary, bedraggled crew went below decks, back to bailing.

I thought to myself, 'So THIS is yachting!'

Analyzing our circumstances, we couldn't do any more than sail her as easy as possible for the closest land and beach her—if no aid was available. We were stretching our strength, and her ability to hold together and float . . . another type of yacht race!

Night would soon be upon us. The wind was building fast and the yacht was working, creaking and groaning. The sounds played on my mind as I steered her through seas; up and over and under great masses of water. I watched and watched along the decks, and felt she was twisting, as well as beginning to hog and sag. It was an awful feeling, perhaps exaggerated by the sounds. Perhaps! Could I be hallucinating?

The hatch slid open. Out came the owner. He was still very drunk. His face in the diminished light was vicious. He came back to the helm on my left side and braced himself on the wheelbox.

"Howdy," I said.

He stuck his face into mine, his foul breath reeking with days of drinking. "Adams, you don't like me, do you?"

"We are all exhausted," I said. "Why don't you turn in and get some sleep?"

He repeated, "You don't like me, do you?" With that he doubled up his fist and brought his arm back.

I quickly decided that if he swung, I would bring my left leg up hard, swing hard at his face with the butt of my left hand and try to guard my jaw with my right hand. It was awkward in a sitting position, but my choices were restricted. If we went into a clinch, it would be bad; we could go over the side and never be found. The fellows below would not know with the slamming, crashing, and banging of the seas.

God's timing was perfect. Just as more hell was about to break loose the hatch slid open—it was the right guy! Frank stuck his head out and said, "Skipper, what do you need?"

The winches for trimming the storm trysail were opposite the wheel box on the deck.

"Frank, haul in on the trysail."

This brought Frank, who disliked this man so completely, within one foot of him. Frank seemed to sense the scene and his presence eased the tension. The owner stumbled back to the hatch, waded into his cabin, and locked the door. Frank calmly trimmed the trysail . . . a quarter of an inch!

The black morning of the fifth day at 0300 hours was moonless and bleak. Cold, wet, and keeping the bilge pumps going incessantly, we were beat. I prayed hard. Looking out and around at the horizon my prayers were answered—a faint light far at sea on the horizon! It came and went, mostly went, with the lumpy seas. I looked hard, wanting it to be real. When I was sure, I called, "All hands on deck—light on the horizon on the port quarter aft!" They all scrambled up—hope beating eternal within grim faces after our nights of despair.

"Fellows, we have only one flare left. We must vote whether to use it. It is your lives and your flare. Do we fire it?"

They voted, "Fire it."

Into the wind at 45 degrees I pointed the loaded Very pistol to give the ball of red fire and its parachute a ride as high as possible. Hopefully it would stay up and ride the updrafts off of the big seas as long as possible. Bang! That flare rode high on our prayers and stayed up for a quarter of a mile riding the gale wind before it hit the water. It was the most beautiful flare I had ever seen. We all watched the little light way out at sea, perhaps five miles away. It was difficult to judge the distance in the lumpy seas and darkness.

A long five minutes went by. It seemed like an hour. "Please."

If the crew on that vessel had seen our flare, the helmsman may have to be authorized to change course, which would take some time if the officer in command was not on the bridge—if it was a ship.

The light seemed to stop—then I realized the vessel must have been turning approximately 90 degrees to head toward us. As it came bow on, its two white range lights, one high forward and one higher aft, became obvious. Through the binoculars I could see her red and green running lights. What a thrill that was! We were shaking. My teeth chattered. My hands were blue and numb.

Predawn light was upon us. Through the glasses she appeared to be a freighter and coming with a bone in her teeth—rolling violently. In about 40 minutes she was within an eighth of a mile of us as the dawn broke. She changed course to circle us 300 feet off.

I gulped as I read her name on the bow. It was the *Sun Yat Sen* out of China. We spoke no Chinese!

What a relief it was as they closed in, rolling and pitching, when an officer on the bridge called out downwind through a megaphone in good broken Chinese-English, "What do you need?"

Sun Yat Sen
16mm photo by Al Adams, Skipper, 1946
(note rolled up chart on right center edge)

"We are in sinking condition!" was my reply through a rolled up soggy chart Frank had rescued.

"Stand by," he said as they continued to circle us. He left the wing of the bridge. Four minutes later he hurried out and said, "Ahoy, I have contacted the Coast Guard at Cherry Point. They are on their way."

All of the fellows gave forth yells of relief and gratitude, all but the owner who was mad and miserable.

He said to us in his drunken stupor, "I don't want any part of this. We don't need any help. This is the finest yacht ever built."

The officer again called over. "I have given the Coast Guard your latitude and longitude. Try to hold your position. Do you need anything? Can you stay afloat?"

We needed the feel of land at this moment.

Tired as the freighter looked, she was the best looking ship I had ever seen. I debated for a moment with myself, knowing they run on a tight schedule, then decided they had made possible our rescue, help must be coming. I called over and told him we would wait for the Coast Guard. I released him with much thanks. He waved, wished us luck and sailed away. It was lonely watching the propeller lift out and then slap the seas, burying as she disappeared over the horizon heading north by east.

We had a new shot of adrenalin and though exhausted, we bailed. I administered more water and codeine to Sam who looked very bad. I thought of getting him on the freighter but he was too ill to take those rough seas in a small skiff. Better, perhaps, to wait for the Coast Guard. We were now in the Gulf Stream, which was setting two to three knots northward. The northerly gale eased a bit through the day. I estimated that in order to hold our position, I would have to keep *Vayu* on a course into the Gulf Stream and thus we might better keep our position, equalizing our boat speed with the set of the Gulf Stream current.

We got rest and food, spelling each other on the buckets and the manual wobble pump. Mort kept the electric bilge pump going by keeping the generator droning away, getting the water down to four sloshing inches over the cabin sole. In her length that was still too much water but it seemed with all bailing methods going, that was the best we could do.

We watched the horizon all day but nothing came to us. We waited and bailed. As evening came on, the owner hit the juice as usual behind his locked cabin door. He still wanted no part of this action. Frank lit a kerosene light to show 360° around the horizon as night engulfed us. We felt certain help would arrive at least by sun up. All night we kept our routine going. The morale was waning as morning came after a sinister night of high velocity squalls that kept the helmsman and bailers busy.

Thirty hours went by, when into our sky came a PBM flying boat. What a sight!! The best-looking plane I had ever seen—beautiful!

Coast Guard Plane—PBM Flying Boat
Photo from 16mm film taken by Skipper Al Adams—1946

It was a Coast Guard plane. The pilot waved as he put the big bird over the tip of the mainmast. He circled us for three minutes then came over us again. One of his crew tossed a fluttering yellow object out of a window. It hit the water 200 feet from *Vayu*. The fellows got the skiff into the water and tied 250 feet of line to her painter. If the skiff capsized, hopefully they could pull it back. With my life jacket double checked, I jumped in and rowed to the object. It was a wooden shaped bottle 10" long by 2" by 2" with square corners. It was painted vibrant yellow and attached was a yellow piece of cloth 10" wide and 36" long. In one end of the wooden bottle was a cork. I retrieved the floating unit, removed the cork and pulled out a sheet of notebook-sized paper rolled up tight.

It was an unusual message made up of questions, the answers would be by pantomime using the placement of crewmembers on deck to tell our story.

Questions:

1. Is your engine inoperable? If so, have one man stand on the afterdeck.
2. Is someone sick? If so, have two men stand amidships.
3. If you need food or water have one man stand on the foredeck.

I rowed back close to the yacht and called to Dick to stand on the afterdeck. He responded quickly. I then called to Frank and Mort to stand amidships.

The pilot brought the big bird in over us again and dipped his wing that he understood.

As yet, he didn't know of our plight—that we were sinking. As I clambered from the skiff to the deck, I called to the fellows to hurry below, fill the buckets with water and hand them up to me.

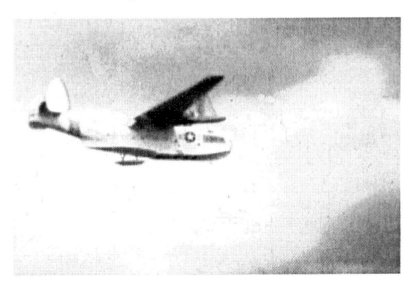

Coast Guard Plane—PBM Flying Boat
Photo from 16mm film taken by Skipper Al Adams—1946

I waved to the plane to approach us again. As he buzzed us, the pilot banked, then squared away from us approximately a half mile off. I tossed the water from the buckets over the side, keeping an eye on the plane coming in toward us.

The pilot was hep, he dipped his wing and circled out for another three minutes. Then, in he came close to the masts and down fluttered another yellow streamered wooden bottle. Frank held the painter as I got in the skiff and rowed to the floating bottle. The message read, "Understand yacht is taking on water. Can you keep her afloat for ten hours? It will take that long for the Coast Guard Cutter to get to you. If you can keep up with it, have one man stand on the foredeck."

I called to Mort to hurry to the foredeck. The plane was making its approach and again dipped his wing. As he went over this time a yellow streamered bottle came down attached to a package. The bombardier up there was doing a great job, for each time the object he dropped landed within two hundred feet, and this last splashdown was seventy-five feet from the *Vayu*.

Back on deck we opened a waxed, watertight box 8" x 8" x 12". It contained a single, spring-loaded Very pistol and ten flares. The latest note read, "Understand you are in a sinking condition. It is too rough for us to land. You indicate you will attempt to keep her afloat until the Cutter arrives. Fire a flare every hour through the night. Keep as much light going as possible. Hold your position close as you can. Your latitude and longitude has been reported. We are low on fuel and must return to the base. Good luck!"

We lifted the skiff and secured it in its deck chocks.

As the sun went down we had renewed life. We bailed, ate fruit salad, bailed, and took more guff from the owner.

He, being in an alcoholic world, wanted no part of this aid, or our water world and kept mumbling, "This is the finest yacht in the world and she doesn't need a rescue."

He was a menace and becoming increasingly more belligerent. Frank bristled and I was concerned they would tangle. Aside, I told Frank, "I understand thoroughly, but don't let anything happen if you possibly can control it. But if he attacks, then defend yourself."

Sam was a big concern. I gave him lots of water and aspirin, which was all that was left. The medicine kit was ruined.

From the galley, we took the largest metal cooking pot with a wire bail and into it I poured a quart of kerosene, a quart of crankcase oil and mixed in some rags Mort had saved from his engine room operation. To try to keep light that night to aid a rescue, we lashed the bail of the two-gallon size pot to the aft end of the mizzen boom and topped it up ten feet off the water. At 2000 hours we lit the mixture that made great light. The fire was less apt to scorch the yacht out there. The building wind blew the flame wildly for two hours then along came a huge sea and engulfed the entire afterdeck. That big sea ripped our big pot off the mizzen boom and Davy Jones' Locker got our pot.

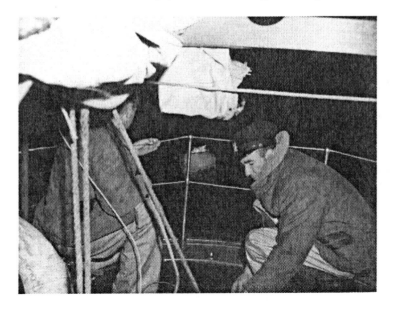

Illuminating rigging to signal location for USCG Cutter rescue.
Photo by Al Adams, Skipper

Vayu was tacked every hour on the hour, and as we came about a flare was fired hourly throughout the rest of the night. Dawn came and went—we bailed. That afternoon late, gale winds hammered us. All night it blew. We tacked and bailed. It was hard to hold our position but we tried. The Coast Guard flares were down to one. We kept our red eyes, smarting and burning from exposure and salt, on the horizon—one man on watch, the rest bailing.

At 1000 hours the next morning the drone of a plane brought us alive. The PBM was back. We waved wildly as he buzzed us. The plane circled us, and then began an odd maneuver, which later made sense. The pilot started a huge expanding circle, or spiral, increasing his distance from *Vayu* as the center. At intervals the plane dropped floating smoke flares on the ocean. The spiral pattern took the plane over the horizon—out of sight, with 15 visible smoke clouds encircling us. The smoke was to help the PBM crew keep track of us.

One hour went by as we watched the sky on that bumpy horizon.

"There she is!"

The plane came straight at us from the Southeast. We ducked, for it looked like she would hit the masts but the pilot pulled up, held his course and continued past us for approximately three miles. All of his tactics were for a purpose. I had a hunch he was guiding a vessel toward us and was showing the way. Possibly his radio or one on a surface vessel was not operable and the pilot was doing his job visually.

I took a quick bearing to get his course and said, "Fellows, keep watching to the southwest by south a quarter south. If my hunch is right we will see a ship on that bearing."

The plane did a reciprocal course back over us and took off on southwest by south a quarter south. Almost out of sight he banked sharply and returned to the course he originally held to pick us up. With the binoculars Dick picked up a vessel. In twenty minutes the best looking craft I had ever seen came skidding to a stop sixty-five feet from us. What a thrill that was to see—a 95' Coast Guard Cutter.

The officer on the bridge waved and called out through his megaphone, "What do you need first?" His crew was bustling about the decks anticipating their first orders.

"Sir, you fellows look great. Thanks! Would you shoot me a Handy Billy?" (Simple long-lift bilge pump).

"Fire the Lyle gun," he shouted.

The crew responded by firing the shot line between our masts. We pulled in the light linen line to which was attached a half-inch line, and tied onto that line was a 6' long galvanized Handy Billy. Dick started pumping it by putting the suction end down the main hatch. We could stay on deck and pump. Next, attached to the half-inch line was a three-inch hawser. We brought the end of the big hawser over the bow, wrapped it three times around the base of the mainmast, and carried the bitter end forward, belaying it to the anchor windlass. We wrapped sail bags around the hawser where it would chafe on the head stay fitting. With three-quarter inch line, Frank tied on the chafing pieces around the hawser and at the same time secured the covered hawser to the head stay fitting. This was to reduce its chance of wear.

An officer on the bridge called over to apologize for the long delay in getting to us. "Two cutters were sent out. The other one got swamped with a big sea and had to limp back two days ago. Our radar, radio, and direction finder washed out so we couldn't pick you up. We were forty miles from you. It is a good thing the PBM came out and got us together. Do you have a radio?"

"Radio washed out," I replied. "The yacht is full of sea water. We have a hurt crewman. We have bailed for five days."

"Here we go," he said. "Signal if you need help."

The cutter eased off and tightened the towline. We checked the manner we had secured. It was holding. We gave the all-okay signal and away we went.

They had been out here taking a beating looking for us the hard way. We appreciated that for we had been out here looking for them—the hard way!

Coast Guard Cutter—setting up tow line
Photo from 16mm film taken by Skipper Al Adams—1946

We were totally unnerved, shivering, relieved, but near-exhaustion really got to us causing a let down. Adrenalin was short, but not for long! We pulled out on the end of a 600-foot towline at four knots, five, six, seven, eight, nine, ten, eleven, twelve knots of speed. We were in trouble! We were exceeding our hull speed and being sucked under. The entire afterdeck went under and water poured below through the main hatch. The fellows scrambled out—yelling as they closed the hatch to keep the rush of water from filling her up.

The cutter was six hundred feet ahead of us rolling and tossing. The towline was dragging through two big sea crests between us to keep from jerking the towline. I had little time to get them stopped for the water in that short span was over our bunks amidships. I grabbed the flare pistol, shoved in the last flare and sent it up. It worked. Someone was watching. The cutter stopped and brought us close with their power windlass on their afterdeck.

Coast Guard Cutter towing *Vayu*
Photo from 16mm film taken by Skipper Al Adams—1946

I called over and explained we were exceeding our hull speed and were about to go under. This is a fundamental of a displacement hull that is not true of a planing type hull; therefore, these young Coast Guard fellows possibly were not aware that the drag on the wetted surface of the deep-keeled hull was sucking *Vayu* under. She was working and tired, and water poured into her and over her with this speed. If we were to save her, it had to be on her terms.

I called, "If I flash a light in the night, please check us."

Our arms and backs ached but still we had to continue bailing. It was difficult on the helm with so much water in the hull. She didn't want to track with the Cutter. She would yaw away from the course in spite of the rudder positioning and caused violent jerks from the towline.

Away we went into the night at four knots. At midnight, I could feel that with the change of the watch, the new throttle man eased her up to six knots. I flashed the beam light. They pulled us up close again.

"Sir, we can't keep up with the water coming into the hull if we exceed four knots."

"Okay," the new officer of the bridge sang out. "We will keep our speed down. See you in the morning."

We spelled each other bailing and steering that night, all day and all the next night. That next morning it was obvious that we were closing in on the shore. The water was gray-yellow and murky. Fog was setting in. The seas flattened out. The wind went light. As the day came on we couldn't see land but I was sure our keel smelled it. Again, I wasn't sure these young fellows on the Cutter realized we drew at least fifteen feet. This water is getting shallow! Then I saw one hundred feet to starboard a row of narrow poles sticking up out of the water, which had been placed there by local fishermen to mark shallow water. I got the Cutter's attention and informed them how deep we were in the water. The skipper was most appreciative and when I pointed over to the poles sticking up, he gulped!

Both vessels were nearly aground. The Cutter swung to port and went back out to sea about two miles and then bore off to starboard to get more southing. He wasn't too sure of his position, coming in by the seat of his pants— dead reckoning. He made another turn, hard to starboard. His bow watch had spotted a channel marker west of us. We turned and passed the marker close aboard, then proceeded on a course to pick up the next channel marker. We continued far too long. The next marker didn't loom up. I spotted more sticks in the water ahead to starboard at the same time they did, for they stopped abruptly. The propeller wash brought up muddy water. I swung the helm hard to port to escape to deeper water—I hoped!

Cautiously, the Cutter turned to port and proceeded back to the buoy on a reciprocal course. The fog gave us about two hundred and fifty feet of visibility. The Cutter inched up to the buoy bow on. The skipper had the foredeck crew put a line through the big shackle on its top and when the line was secured back on the Cutter, the order was given to reverse engines. To the afterdeck crew, the order was to keep the towline clear of the props. The skipper wanted to prove a point. The buoy moved freely, for it had parted its chain and had floated to the shallows toward Cape Lookout. That was too close. He called to release the buoy. We proceeded south through the fog cautiously—heaving the lead smelling the bottom.

I made a very popular suggestion to my crew: "Get the buckets. Let's throw water over the side instead of pouring it in the cockpit scuppers." This we did.

The skipper of the Cutter understood and had *Vayu* pulled alongside. Big rubber fenders were put between the vessels. Bow and stern lines, and fore and aft spring lines, properly adjusted, kept the crafts apart as we made way, hopefully, to find the channel into Beaufort, North Carolina. The fog thickened. My idea of throwing the bucketfuls of water over the side paid off. The skipper came aboard *Vayu* to look below and assess our condition. When he saw the water over the cabin deck and the mess below, he ordered a power driven bilge pump put aboard the yacht.

"Geez," he said, "I had no idea. You guys are really low-key!"

He now knew we had to get her up on her lines to get into the roadstead. We would be lucky not to rub the keel off even with a dry bilge. A gasoline driven pump was readied on *Vayu's* deck by the Cutter crew. A 1½" stream was pumping up out of the main salon and continued for the rest of the trip in.

Everyone breathed easier when the bow watch on the Cutter spotted the next buoy channel marker. The skipper had Sam checked by his Pharmacist Mate who gave him a relaxant and some hot broth. The chef called over and asked what the rest of us would like. It was unanimous: "Hot cocoa." How good it was and we had seconds—and thirds, but no more fruit salad!

We reached the channel enshrouded in fog, the bearing was checked on the chart, and we proceeded in very slowly. Land loomed about us—a breakwater and a sea wall. What a great feeling to be this close. If we had to swim now, the distance to land was shortening.

The owner was most discourteous to the Coast Guard fellows and was his usual miserable self to his crew. We had all saved his yacht and his life. He was to be pitied.

We pulled into the harbor and proceeded to the Coast Guard dock. A big crowd had gathered since word had gotten around town from the crew of the other Cutter, which was washed out after the big wave and had turned back to port.

The Coast Guard fellows on the dock helped us tie up. The impressive thing to me was that the gasoline driven bilge pump they had put on board had pumped a 1-1/2" stream for 5 hours approaching the channel at 2 knots. It was going along with our electric pump and there were still two inches of water over the cabin sole. The big pump was kept on until the bilge water was evacuated. What a mess as all the flotsam settled on the cabin sole, in the passageways, and over the bunks.

Once secure, the officer of the deck had me come aboard and fill out his rescue report with the owner. I officially thanked the Coast Guard personnel for the efficient rescue. They were outstanding. Their next assignment was to go back out and get the channel buoy that was floating free, and take it to the proper location indicated on the chart and attach chain ballast to it.

The Coast Guard report finished, the *Vayu* crew helped Sam ashore. We took him over to the closest bit of earth at his request. He dropped down and kissed the ground— and he meant it.

We took him to the doctor who told him, "You are very lucky you are alive. You have blood in your urine." He taped Sam's ribs and put him to bed. The officer in charge of the base told the owner where the boatyard was located. The yacht would need immediate haul out, and would have to be moved from the Coast Guard dock as soon as possible. They needed the space (besides not wanting it to sink and be a menace to their operations).

Over the phone the yardman talked with the owner and made the appointment. He asked about the yacht's draft. This would be a problem, for high tide would not be until 3 p.m. the next day. She couldn't ride into the railway cradle until high tide.

Back at the boat, the owner had a big audience. He was berating his crew, shouting obscenities, telling the audience his crew had brought the yacht in from sea against his wishes, and that we were rescued when it wasn't necessary. He said, "Look at her lying there. She is beautiful. She is the finest yacht in the world."

Calmly, I explained to the owner that the five of us were very tired; we needed food, and would now move off the boat if he had no further use of us.

He said, "Fine."

We retrieved our wet, soggy gear and phoned for a taxi to take us to a hotel close by. The owner then called over to the crowd and indicated he would like to hire six young men to move aboard and take care of the yacht until the next day. The fellows selected were ready and anxious. They were advised about the bilge pumps and buckets. We cleaned her up below as best we could and the new bailing crew took over.

We went to bed at the local hotel after a dinner of stewed clams, corn bread, and beer at the local cafe. They were the best clams we had ever eaten—everything was the best—we were alive! It was wonderful!

But, an odd occurrence was about to take place. It was sundown as we taxied away leaving the owner with the six volunteers.

After the owner went to a hotel for the night, the new crew decided, "Hey, man, let's get some dates and have a party on the yacht!" They did just that and about midnight, after a great party, the fellows took the girls home and got back to the yacht just before the crack of dawn. When they looked down from the dock, the 76' yacht *Vayu* wasn't there. She had sunk and snapped her dock lines. The water was over the entire hull—her masts were leaning against the dock.

The boatyard sent over a workboat and crew with lifting gear and pumps. After hours of work and using flotation gear, they got her afloat and took her to the ways. When she was raised on the boatyard railway cradle, flat sheets of water poured out of her seams. The yard crew said they didn't understand how we kept her afloat. We didn't either!

It was a close call. Just about as close as was possible in our race for land. Teamwork and the dedication of five fellows, the crew of the Chinese freighter, the crew of the PBM, the crew of the Coast Guard cutter, and the Man upstairs had put it all together. I'd hate for all of us to have to put it all together again. Once was enough for a lifetime!

VAYU's crew topside. (l. to r.) Frank, Mort, Dick and Sam.
Photo by Al Adams, Skipper

Frank in a rare quiet moment. *Photo by Al Adams, Skipper*

Chapter 5

Answers

The foregoing story of this ill-fated voyage was authenticated on a dramatic moving picture taken by the author and shown on the Jack Douglas television program "I Search for Adventure."

I went back the next year and skippered the 80' schooner *Tamarit* from Elizabeth City, North Carolina to California. She drew 9' so I went across Albemarle Sound and down the Inland Waterway to Beaufort, North Carolina. The waterway was dredged to 10 feet.

As I docked at Beaufort, North Carolina, I looked over and there was old *Vayu* tied to the dock. She hadn't been moved in a year and had long masses of growth trailing from her waterline. Her entire bottom had been caulked to get her afloat.

There is more. I went back to Rowayton, Connecticut, on Long Island the same year to skipper the famous 83' schooner *Queen Mab* to California. Harold Vanderbilt formerly owned her and now her new owner had commissioned me to skipper her to California. It was on this cruise, two years later, that I got the answer for the final climax to the *Vayu* saga.

We had sailed the *Queen Mab* out to Bermuda and down to Watling Island through the Windward Passage to Port-au-Prince, Haiti. As guests of the retired former U.S. Ambassador

Queen Mab
Al Adams collection

to Haiti, Horace Ashton, we anchored off his private section
of Arcachon Beach, rather than lie at the busy waterfront of
Port-au-Prince. We were lying a quarter mile off the beach. I
heard a call from ashore, "Ahoy, *Queen Mab!*" The dory was
at our boarding ladder alongside. Into the beach I rowed to
meet a young man who indicated he was on his summer
vacation and could I use a crewman. He seemed to know
boats by his conversation and was impressed with the big
schooner, *Queen Mab.* She was impressive out there at anchor
in that tropical setting. He didn't care where we were going.

One of the California fellows in my crew had married
two weeks before we flew to Connecticut to board the *Queen
Mab.* He was getting homesick for his bride and understandably
so. He had indicated, if I didn't mind, he would fly home,
but would let me know for sure the coming Thursday. He
was a close friend and I understood.

I suggested to the fellow on the beach if he would come back Thursday at 3 p.m., I would have an answer for him. Thursday at 3 p.m. he was back and I signed him on.

Three days later we sailed across the Windward Passage to Guantanamo, Cuba, to haul out at the United States Naval Base and repair the *Queen's* rudder before continuing on across the Caribbean to the Panama Canal.

To learn the extent of the sailing experience of the new crewman, I had him on watch with me. It was a beautiful moonlit night with a 25 mile an hour, balmy trade wind. We chatted about places, people, and finally boats. He mentioned being in the offshore submarine patrol out of the Chesapeake during the war. During our conversation, I mentioned the *Vayu* cruise.

He came right back, "You don't mean the 76' ketch?" We were surprised to find we had sailed the same vessel. "But," he said, "if you knew what I knew you would never have gone to sea in her."

What I was about to learn was the answer I needed, for it changed my life, putting me on a new tack.

He began, "We had been to sea on *Vayu* about ten days watching for enemy submarines. We got orders to bring *Vayu* back into the Chesapeake for provisions and new orders. It was late on a moonless night. We were in 'black out,' no running lights and no lights on deck. Coming from out at sea, we were just entering the Bay, cautiously, for other vessels would also be without lights. Our windows, skylights, and port lights were painted black and no cigarettes were allowed on deck. I was off watch, and had the cabin on the starboard quarter aft of the main salon." (Note: this was also my cabin on *Vayu.*) "The rest of my off-watch group were in the main salon playing poker. I had been lying down in my bunk but decided to join the others. I got up and opened the cabin door. Then one hell of a crash! I was thrown hard into the main salon. Confusion and panic! The rest of the crew were also thrown violently, taking the gimbaled table with them. I looked back through my cabin door and there was the whole stem and bow of a big Purse Seiner where my bunk used to be. I would have been killed if I hadn't gotten up.

"The helmsman of the seiner was a smart fellow. Instead of getting excited and reversing his engine, he reduced speed to about one knot, keeping the bow of the seiner hard into the ketch. He gave orders to secure the vessels tight together, and get the pumps going so that *Vayu* wouldn't sink. In that attitude, we eased along until dawn. At first light of day the seiner pushed *Vayu* to a shipyard, kept the pumps going and got her hauled out.

"Surveyors were called immediately, for the Navy wanted *Vayu* back in service at once, if she was salvageable. Work orders were written for the yard to replank her in that gaping hole and permitted them to use short planks instead of extending the planks from all the way aft at least to amidships. So she was very weak aft of amidships on the starboard side. The new planks were not long enough nor were they alternated long and short for strength, as this is vital. Further," he said, "it was discovered that *Vayu* was originally constructed with a large cypress wood lined ice chest forward of amidships. Through the years, ice was carried in this compartment to aid in preserving food and the chilling of drinks but during those years of use and aided by poor ventilation, ice water dripping down caused the cypress to rot. The water and rot spore then made its way to infect the yacht's frames, ceiling, and planks, which were never replaced, and the wood rot spread. As a result, the yacht was weakened on the port side forward of amidships. There were other critical things that were revealed but suffice it to say the yacht built so long ago was not seaworthy and as the years progressed she became even less sea capable. The cypress liner had been removed years ago, but the damage to the hull beneath the liner had not been repaired."

This conversation was most valuable. With the added weight in *Vayu* of the new and filled 100-gallon gasoline tank, the huge bank of heavy submarine type batteries, the large generator, the teak doghouse aft of amidships in the area of the short planks, and with a ton of lead pigs stowed forward over the stem adjacent to the rotted frames and planks, it was no wonder she worked, groaned and creaked.

I could see her twist, as I looked down her length, in those vicious Atlantic seas in the whole gale. Amidships, if you sat on her deck planks, she would pinch you. The hull was working and had chewed out the caulking between her planks. Seawater came through her planks, in great areas. It is a wonder *Vayu* and her crew survived.

Three surveyors had not reported the short planks nor the rotted planks and frames. The last surveyor had not indicated the attitude of the yacht with its counter in the water and its bow 24 inches up above the proper waterline. That survey was performed with the yacht in the water, thus there was no excuse for his not reporting this problem.

A disservice was done to the buyer by these reports, extremely expensive to him in many ways. The owner never used the boat again and six of us nearly lost our lives at sea. The Coast Guard crews on the two Cutters were out at sea at great risk and expense, as well as the PBM crew on the flying boat.

As a result of this cruise, and what I had learned, I returned to Southern California determined to become a Marine Surveyor. I apprenticed to a well-known surveyor and boat builder, Stewart Robertson, and took positions in two top yacht maintenance yards, managing one. Eventually, I hung out my shingle, feeling there was a need for the service I could give. For 55 years this has been my profession, and I enjoy it.

An incident occurred as a result of the ill-fated *Vayu* cruise. In 1939, I had studied for and passed the Coast Guard examination as skipper on all navigable waters of the United States. This is a license not readily issued and I had my license on board the *Vayu* where it was ruined in the high water before the yacht sank at the dock in Beaufort, North Carolina. When I returned to California, I went to the office of the Officer in Charge of Marine Inspection in San Pedro and reported the loss. The examining officer said I would have to take the complete examination and physical over again naming the date for the examination, which would take two days. One thing I enjoyed about the Coast Guard examination was that you couldn't bluff it. When taking my first examination, fourteen fellows sat for it and twenty-five minutes after we started the written examination, nine fellows walked out. It was difficult.

I took the physical, the written, and the oral, and turned in my papers. The officer said, "You did very well, best score I have seen. Come with me to the Officer in Charge who will sign your new license."

When I got before this officer, he said to the examining officer, "Why did you have him take this examination over? He sat for it and earned the license years ago in 1939. It is on record here in this office. You should have issued another since he has legitimately lost it."

I spoke up in the man's defense. "Sir, I appreciate that another license could have been issued, but I feel better having this study, review, and update of required material. Thank you both."

It was an adventurous 60 years while that license was being posted in the chart rooms of vessels I captained. It will please me if I can put another 20 years of sea time on that license.

White Death Came Bumping

A Story
of the delivery of the beautiful yacht
Tamarit
from North Carolina to San Diego by way of
the Panama Canal

Shearwater x Tamarit under sail
Photo from Shearwater collection.

Editor's note:
Tamarit was re-named *Shearwater* and is currently owned by Tom Berton. She is berthed in New York's historic harbor and is currently engaged in Corporate and private charters. After sustaining damage from the 911 attack on the World Trade Center, she was recently hauled out, re-fiited and is now back to work in all of her glory. Please visit her website at www.shearwatersailing.com.

WHITE DEATH CAME BUMPING

Maryland's coast was on each side of us as we sailed out from Elizabeth City, North Carolina, for a quick shakedown of the beautiful 80'8" schooner *Tamarit*. She was fresh off the ways and ready for sea—her destination was to be the San Diego Yacht Club at San Diego, California, by way of the Panama Canal.

Tamarit—80′ Schooner
Photo by Al Adams, Skipper—1946

77

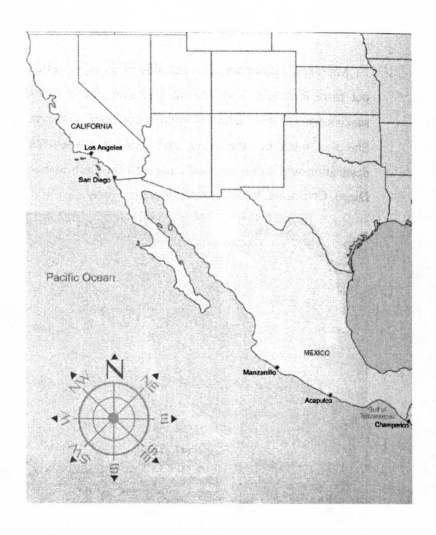

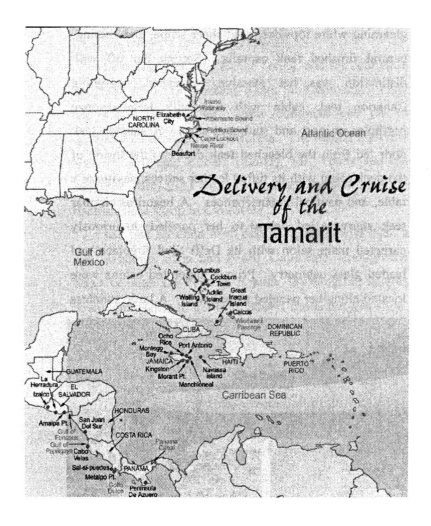

The impressive, capable *Tamarit* awaited with her gleaming white topsides, gold sheer stripe, and shining, natural finished teak caprails. Setting her off with distinction was her massive, varnished, sea-going Rangoon teak cabin with unusually large bronze portholes on port and starboard sides. A staunch teak door led from the bleached teak decks to the inside of the deck cabin with its tufted leather settees, navigator's table, and nautical appurtenances. A beautiful circular teak stairway led below to her paneled, luxuriously carpeted main salon with its Delft tiled fireplace and leaded glass cabinetry. Private appointed cabins were located along her paneled passageway. A large stainless steel galley was forward of the salon. She was invitingly sea-oriented and was named *Tamarit* after a previous owner's estate in Spain.

Tamarit's Rangoon teak cabin with bronze portholes
Photo taken by Jim Delorey—1982

The new owner, Mr. Henry Tenny, and his debutante daughter were from Rancho Santa Fe, California. They had never sailed. Mr. Tenny commissioned me to skipper the schooner to California. The rest of my crew was my wife and Robert Duntley, Mr. Tenny and his daughter. Bob and I had raced actively on board his 32' Pacific Class sloop in California.

I had just returned from delivering the *Dwyn Wen*, a 104' schooner from San Pedro, California, through the Strait of Juan De Fuca to Seattle, Washington, so this new commission to deliver *Tamarit* timed out just right. It would enable me to sail almost all the navigable water around the United States in two trips and as well, the coasts of Middle America and Mexico.

All of us arrived by plane from California, moved on board, provisioned her, and this was our shakedown day to get acquainted with *Tamarit*. She carried a good press of sail, a Marconi main, foresail, Yankee, fisherman, golly wobbler, staysail, jib, outer jib, and genoa.

The shakedown went well and as we powered back into the Elizabeth City yacht basin adjacent to the boat-hauling railway at five knots, I got my first bit of excitement. The docks formed a rectangular cul-de-sac, and 80 feet of water separated the two sides with a dead-end built of solid concrete 180 feet back. As a part of the wharf at the end of the rectangular basin, there was a marine railway leading from the top of the wharf down into the water. This was for hauling boats out of the water in cradles. The cradles rode on the rails, which were typical iron railroad tracks. These rails came down from the wharf and disappeared into the water on about a 22° slant.

Having made the turn into this basin, I was committed, for there was not enough room to turn and go back out. I reduced the throttle and pulled back on the gear control lever so as to dock *Tamarit*. At that instant, a steel bolt in the control linkage dropped out under the cockpit deck making the gearshift useless. A lot of tonnage was moving through the water with no place to escape, for there wasn't enough room to turn and go back out. The engine's gear was still in forward—I could do but one thing. I killed the engine but I was helpless to solve this problem of forward way of five knots. I had barely three seconds to decide what to do and do it. I alerted the crew to brace themselves. To go straight on in, *Tamarit* would crash into the concrete sea wall. That would crush the bowsprit and bow, and might pull the masts down when the jib and head stays would hit the wharf. This would be devastating and embarrassing. There was no time to get an anchor overboard or tell Duntley to open the hatch and go below to find the gear control for reverse.

There was a long chance that flashed in my mind's eye. If I could make a very quick quarter turn of the helm to starboard, and a very fast quarter turn back to port, and God willing, steer her so the lead keel on her bottom might make contact exactly right with the left track of the inclined railroad track of the ways, we might then ride up the track on the yacht's lead keel at the forefoot. This might lift her up, missing her stem, bowsprit, and dolphin striker.

It was unbelievable! The forward edge of the keel was exactly on target and did not slip off that 2½ inch track surface. A surface I could not see five feet under water, discolored by the decaying cypress trees that taint the canal water. *Tamarit*'s bow rose skyward, her bowsprit shooting toward the sky. Had she slipped off the narrow track, her dolphin striker would have struck the railroad ties and the stem would have been crushed.

It was a one-in-a-million occurrence—so beautiful to watch. She slid up about 10 feet and stopped, exposing about three feet of her bottom and waterline stripe. She then slid back down into the basin stern first. No damage was done. The small dent in her lead keel was superficial and was a conversation dent, a future reminder of a great split-second escape. I may have appeared nonchalant and low-key but I was high-key inside. What a relief! Whew! I found the bolt in the bilge where it had fallen and reinstalled it in the gear control linkage so it couldn't fall out.

We sailed the very interesting Inland Waterway traveling in narrow canals, rivers, the Albemarle Sound, Pamlico Sound, Neuse River, and Adams Creek. It was pleasant under full sail on a close to broad reach in narrow, winding channels with beautiful farms, pastures with cows grazing, flowers to the water's edge, villages and many, many drawbridges. The channels were dredged to ten to fourteen feet. By following the chart and the unique channel marking system very closely, we were able to avoid the shallows. Traveling at night was totally discouraged as commercial barges and tugs could be encountered, and in the narrows it would make navigation dangerous. Turnout areas and areas for anchoring for the night were indicated on the charts.

The limited dredged depths were a constant concern, for *Tamarit* drew nine feet. We rubbed bottom many times but never were we aground. The water was coffee colored, from the decaying cypress of the dismal swamp areas that fed into the waterway. We passed many local people sitting contentedly fishing for mullet, trout, and flounder. The drawbridge operators were friendly and opened the gates on signal with our proper number of blasts on the foghorn. They would take the name of the yacht and write it in their log as we moved through. It was fun timing our approach to the opening bridges by flattening our sails or luffing them to reduce our speed so as to move through as the bridges opened. The operators then closed the bridges for automobile and foot traffic. However, it could have been embarrassing if we misjudged, and left masts and sails hanging on the bridge. By sailing the inland waterway we could avoid sailing outside around Cape Hatteras—the graveyard of ships. I have been that route.

The Inland Waterway's aids to navigation are well done. It is helpful, if anticipating this waterway, to first become acquainted with the system. Sailing as we were under full sail with the wind fair, it proved beneficial to have one person following the chart and the marker system, and the helmsman receiving the information for buoy numbers and course changes. A bow watch and another crew person with the lead and line handy kept the crew busy and interested. The remaining crew kept cameras operating. Some drawbridge operators walked around capstans and with their one-man power, opened and closed the bridges.

On Albemarle Sound we experienced a vicious squall that made up astern of us. It was black and menacing. Fortunately, I looked back to see those black, torn, low clouds. I called all hands to drop the mainsail and the jib. The gaskets were barely secured around the furled sails when the squall struck; with it came flashing lightning and thunder. Under the foresail alone we fairly flew before the squall and the horizontal, stinging rain.

I often reflect back on that experience of traveling the Inland Waterway under sail. Friendly people along the canals and riverbanks called out telling us how beautiful *Tamarit* looked under full sail as we glided by. Often the banks were so close in the canals that we could converse with the people without raising our voices.

A curving, twisting waterway with so much to see; a changing panorama, seldom experienced hour after pleasant hour under sail. It came to an end at Beaufort, North Carolina, a great little sea-goers' town near Beaufort Inlet, established in 1709.

It was at Beaufort the year before that I had left the old ketch *Vayu* on which my crew and I nearly lost our lives. That was a never to be forgotten saga at sea of bailing five days and nights to stay afloat. We made it in to Beaufort but *Vayu* sank at the dock. She was refloated and taken to the boatyard where her bottom was totally recaulked. She was still there tied up at the dock. After a short visit with her, our laundry refreshed, water replenished in our tanks, we were away on *Tamarit*, out into the Atlantic and the Gulf Stream—destination California. Our cruise now would be by way of the Spanish Main where lies the constant lure and inspiration of sailor adventurers.

Below Cape Lookout we departed the waterway for the open sea and laid a course for Watling Island, San Salvador, in the Bahamas. Columbus landed on this island when he discovered the West Indies. That was an eventful day—October 12, 1492. There is a rough coral stone monument on the lonely beach to commemorate Columbus' landing. Thinking back on my days at sea, it has been great fun to stand at the historic locations made famous by the boatmen of the past. I have transited the Panama Canal seven times. During one passage I went to the spot where Balboa had stood and where he climbed a tree to first set eyes on the Pacific Ocean. He waded into the Pacific after descending from the tree and "claimed for Spain all the lands the Pacific washed." Balboa's grave has been absorbed by the jungle and lost to mankind.

Once I sailed into Porto Bello, a sleepy little bight on the Caribbean side of Panama. It carries many memories with its ruined walls, rusted cannons of colonial times and the memories of Sir Francis Drake who was buried at sea outside the bay. This was another place plundered by Sir Henry Morgan, the pirate.

One time I stood on the lonely island of San Miguel, off the California coast, where Cabrillo, the Portuguese navigator, died and was buried under the shifting, windswept sands. His, too, is a lost grave. I also sailed to the lonely little island in the Philippines where the natives killed Magellan in the surf. Now, I was to stand at the spot where Columbus first set foot on the New World. There have been many more but those four were especially important to me.

Another time I stood on the shore of secluded, tropical Espirito Santo at beautiful Hog Harbor in the New Hebrides and thought reverently of my great friend, Harry Pigeon, who sailed his yawl *Islander* twice around the world single-handed. It was on the reef here that his next little yawl, a 26-foot version of the 34-foot *Islander,* was wrecked during Harry's attempt to sail around the world the third time. Harry never sailed again after that. His last attempt was with Vera Rideout of California and also Harry's bride, Margaret Gardiner, whom he met on his first trip around the world when he put in at Gardiner's Island on Long Island Sound. Margaret's father owned the island. Harry never forgot Margaret. Many years went by and he made another cruise around the world before he sent for her. They were married in San Pedro, California—she was in her 70's and Harry in his 80's. I had the pleasure of sailing with Harry; he stayed often at my home and I took their wedding photographs on board his yawl. They were a great sailing couple. I visited the Hog Harbor coconut plantation of Mr. Graziano. I learned he was the man who took Harry, Margaret and Vera in off the beach and cared for them after their little yawl was wrecked on the reef so far from California. Mr. Graziano had had no contact through the years, since the wreck, with anyone that sailed to this remote area.

Harry had once said to me in answer to my question, "Why do you make these circumnavigations alone?"

"Well," he said, "I like people but it's difficult to live in tight quarters with them so I just go it alone."

He had two people with him this last trip.

"The girls," Mr. Graziano said, "swayed Harry into sailing into the narrow opening of beautiful Hog Harbor so that they could wash some clothes." Harry told Graziano that his chart of this end of Espirito Santo was poor and inaccurate on depth. Perhaps the growing coral made it shallow. A hurricane struck and the yawl was totally wrecked on the reef.

When I was there, I found many fresh water springs in the coral and sand beaches. It was ideal for drinking, washing clothes and bathing. I swam in the surf and then knelt on the beach to drink the fresh spring water and wash off the salt. Evidently Harry's sailing directions for this area mentioned the fresh water springs, thus the ladies' desire to go in to freshen up and wash clothes. So few boatmen seem to sail to the New Hebrides. It is a fascinating cruising area, so many lush tropical islands with primitive people, volcanoes, and Nambus tribes, wild boar and fine coves. I enjoyed every minute cruising through these islands.

The *President Coolidge,* a cruise ship of the American President Line, hit a mine near Espirito Santo during World War II and sank. She lies there on the bottom on an incline, her bow higher than her stern. We got in close and sailed over the sunken ship. We could see it below our keel. Later, while walking along the beach at Santo, I came upon a very simple concrete slab with this inscription:

In Memory Of
Captain Edward J. Euart
103rd Field Artillery Battalion, USA
October 26, 1942

This inscription interested me because of its location away on the beach in the vicinity of the sunken *President Coolidge.* I met a local Briton who informed me that Captain Euart rescued many of his crew that were thrown into the water by the explosion. He made many trips swimming out to save them. Finally, exhausted, he drowned.

To pick up our story again on board *Tamarit;* we laid our course from Beaufort, North Carolina, on a port tack for San Salvador in the Bahamas, British West Indies, approximately 635 nautical miles to the south on a line with the eastern tip of Cuba. Watches were assigned—two girls for galley duty was a luxury and when they wished, they could stand wheel watches. It was a good system on a beautiful yacht under fair skies. The wind was balmy at 15 knots, a solid trade-wind feel, and the sea was sparkling in the midday sun.

The unmistakable great deep blue Gulf Stream moves north like a huge river within the ocean. By its color, its warm temperature and the strands of gulf weed it carries, it is instantly obvious when one enters the stream. We could see the current whip, the intense color demarcation and already our taffrail log rotator towing 60 feet astern was beginning to foul in the floating gulf weed. Unfouling the rotator was no problem. It is well to notice it in time or the distance traveled by the yacht over the bottom is not going to be accurate in plotting the dead reckoned position. Sailing south against the Gulf stream as it sets northward gives an over-reading due to the three to four knot velocity of the stream. This should be accounted for in assuming the vessel's position.

Bob suggested, "Let's go swimming!" The air was quite warm. The decks were hot and the lunch had settled, so why not? We were sailing under main, foresail, staysail, and jib. So I trimmed her out with jib and main flattened to slow the schooner, and let the fores'l close up and jib trimmed ease her along at four knots. A length of 1/2" line 40' long was trailed astern with a few knots tied in the aft end to aid our grip when being towed through the water. The Jacobs ladder was put over the transom to aid us in climbing in and out of the water. The two ladies decided not to swim. My wife took the helm. That proved to be very fortunate for me.

It was one, two, three, go! as Bob and I dove off the bowsprit together, both on the port side. We would swim with lots of high energy along the length of the yacht and the first to reach the line trailing astern would receive an IOU for an ice cream cone when we got to a place between here and California that served them. It was Bob's ice cream cone the first trip. Then I evened the score and cancelled out the cones. We hung on the towline and just let *Tamarit* pull us along. Little did we realize how attractive we were kicking, swimming and diving. We climbed aboard and went to the foredeck then out on the bowsprit and this time Bob said, "One, two, three, go!" I dove but he held onto the jib stay and stayed on the bowsprit. Not realizing he had not dived, I turned on the splash fest to get to the line first and perhaps win a chit on an ice cream cone. Maybe I could take delivery of it in Kingston, Jamaica, Panama, or Nicaragua.

Just as I surfaced, I was bumped on my right hip. Certain it was Bob I started my Australian crawl. As I exhaled under the water's surface, I looked straight down and there was the "bumper," a huge shark. It turned on its side and looked straight at me perhaps 12 feet below in that beautiful deep blue Gulf Stream. A vicious, threatening countenance it had, with its open mouth and that awful eye. But there was beauty in his shape and the way he fit this environment. Odd how many thoughts one has in a split second. One of my most immediate thoughts, however, was escape. Sharks are said to be sending warnings when they bump with their noses with an open mouth. Certainly this Great White Shark was warning as he came bumping! If he was trying to scare me, he was successful!

As Dr. H. David Baldridge, a scientist for the U.S. Navy, has said, "Sharks may react this way because the swimmer unwittingly has interrupted a courting procedure, has trespassed on the shark's territory or cut off its escape route." If I had done any of these I was sorry. But right now he was coming fast, straight for me, jaws open and to hell with my apology.

Mr. Reg Bragonier wrote, "If menaced by a shark, remain as still as possible, indicating that you are neither interesting nor threatening. If it remains nearby, face it intelligently; put your head in the water and watch it carefully. If it hunches its back, wags its head and begins swimming stiffly from side to side, assume that it is screaming at you to leave. Do so quietly. If it begins making aggressive passes at you, do whatever you can to ward it off and scare it away. Scream at it, pummel it, and kick at it with your feet. As a last resort, gouge its eyes and gills with your bare hands. But do something—anything—to fight back. The odds are four-to-one in your favor that activity on your part will have some beneficial effect."

What I did at that moment was all I could do—what the three on the deck did, saved my life.

The girls were standing amidships on the port side, looking down watching the swim meet. Both of them had seen this one-act shark drama and they screamed, "SHARK!" Bob ran to where they were as I shot up and grabbed the varnished cap rail. Every muscle in my body was trying to pull the lower half of my torso out of the water. My legs and feet came up. My left hand, being wet, slipped off the smooth varnished cap rail just as good old Bob's hands grabbed my wrists and pulled me straight up with the shark slamming his big jaws right at my feet, so close my toes touched his nose and the clash of his jaws vibrated through my body.

The shark seemed disappointed having his lunch interrupted. He looked up and swam close to the side of the hull, back to the taffrail log line and the rotator. I had watched a shark swallow my taffrail log rotator while sailing off the south shore of Cuba on another cruise. Rotators are important and I didn't want to lose another. So, I ran aft and pulled on the log line as fast as I could, hand over hand. As fast as I pulled, the shark went after the metal rotator, biting and clashing his jaws at the evasive spinner, but the rotator was saved.

Lashed to the running backstay was my 1,000-yard fishing reel and split cane rod. The line was 108-pound test and carried a heavy stainless steel leader, a heavy-duty swivel and a heavy trolling lure. Zane Grey had set four world's records with this gear many years prior. For writing a story about some of his Australian fishing successes off the Great Barrier Reef, the equipment was presented to me—one of my proud possessions. I grabbed the rod and cast the lure in the shark's territory and he took it! Bob helped me into my harness and zing went the reel as the line screamed out. Bob put *Tamarit* into the wind to slow her and I went to work—gaining and losing line, gaining and losing! He fought impressively.

Before leaving Elizabeth City, I bought an old oak office chair and cut the legs off, leaving short, strong 10-inch stumps. I always carry a pole butt gimbal for steadying the fishing rod while fighting a sizeable fish. This gimbal had been attached firmly to the forward edge of the chair seat before we sailed. The chair was on the afterdeck. I dropped into the seat, placed the butt of the pole into the socket of the gimbal. Now I was ready with harness, gimbal and strong fish fighting equipment.

The shark sounded with my lure then he shot to the surface, he headed for England and then China. For an hour and forty-five minutes, he fought. I wasn't sure who was going to win this battle. My wife kept pouring bucketfuls of seawater over me to keep me cooled off. Then for another thirty minutes the shark sounded and hung heavily on the line, not giving an inch. I kept the line taut and finally his nose must have started up. I kept reeling in, inch by hard earned inch, until he broke the surface. Bob dropped the mainsail. A line was looped around the shark's tail and attached to the main halyard. We winched him up over the rail for pictures. He was fighting mad, violent and weighed 510 pounds. We lowered him back in his environment, hoping I had not interrupted his courting procedure. The moving picture of this episode was shown on the Jack Douglas television program "Golden Voyage."

Tamarit was in her element. She completed the picture as only a schooner can when seen sailing on the horizon.

Blue skies from horizon to horizon, whitecaps on the emerald sea and her quickly healed wake boiling off to show her path as she reached for the island of Columbus, San Salvador.

It was 0600 when I spotted the flash of the Watling Lighthouse. A perfect time to make our landfall after a beautiful sunrise and a great sail. The low-lying, sandy island is only 140 feet at its highest point; that was on the far side, making it difficult to see this island from out at sea. Columbus arrived here the hard way—with no chart, no lighthouse and with his crew expecting to drop off the edge of their flat sea world. Mine was a British Admiralty chart developed from soundings made in 1898. It had interesting notations such as "Do not trust the depth over the reefs for the coral may be growing." In the years since the soundings, it wasn't for certain if the coral had all good growing years. If so, we did what we must and threw the lead as we reduced sail down to the foresail, proceeded slowly and cautiously—smelling the bottom.

We timed our arrival to drop anchor just after 0800 to give the people of Cockburn Town time to arise and get about. These people are of African descent and there were only a few people on the island. They were interesting, kindly, friendly, and very poor. They spoke very good, correct, Oxford English, like east end London, displaced and so remote.

From seaward, where we anchored an eighth of a mile off the white sand beach, we could see the spire of tile Roman Catholic Church freshly whitewashed. On a pole was a pale light we had watched as we sailed out of the darkness into the sunrise. There was no town here as such. It is known as Riding Rock Settlement or Cockburn Town. A little pier jutted out from the beach to receive the mail schooner, which calls once a month. By now, most all the people in the little settlement were on the pier. Unbelievably clear water extended out to us. *Tamarit* seemed suspended over the white sand bottom. Sitting in the dinghy, twenty feet away, one could see the entire bottom of the boat and her keel. The sandy bottom, four fathoms below, was in clear detail. The light reflecting up from the white sugar sand bottom through the emerald water made *Tamarit* a soft, beautiful green instead of white.

We raised the British Merchant flag at our starboard main spreader signal hoist and below it the yellow quarantine flag. At the stern, we flew the American flag on the staff. Almost simultaneously, a small Bahamian boat put out through the mild surf carrying the Commissioner in his all-whites and pith helmet. With him was the Constable and two boys, one to scull, the other to bail. So few boats had ever sailed to this little island that we got an immediate welcome. They liked the yacht and our Scotch, and the boys enjoyed cookies and candy bars. Watling was formerly the island of Guanahami, and being remote, the islanders enjoyed people from distant places. I brought out our pilot charts to orient them, for they didn't know where California was. They didn't know the shape of their little island and they didn't realize that their little Watling Island was but one of the 3,000 islands in their little archipelago which extends 500 miles to the northeast of Cuba.

The original inhabitants of the island, whom Columbus called Lucayans or Arawaks, were later transported by their Spanish conquerors to work as slaves in the mines of Cuba and Haiti. Man again interrupted a small peaceful world while discovering, but causing destruction.

We were quickly cleared with no formalities and no charges. We brought down the quarantine flag; we were welcome to go ashore.

I mentioned to the Commissioner about the close call I had with the shark on our sail down. He looked shocked and, shaking his head back and forth, said, "Nobody swims in de Gulf Stream."

The boys asked if they could come back and bring others. Soon we had thirty of all ages. We brought out an old wind-up phonograph and played music. They danced and sang to our music. Then I asked one of the young boys if he knew about Christopher Columbus and his men who came to their island along ago from Spain on the *Niña, Pinta* and *Santa Maria*. It was a great moment for us and it was their cue, for they immediately broke forth in good voice. Weeping unashamedly, they sang their anthem of the Admiral Columbus who sailed to their island. It was a touching highlight to be in that island setting with these gracious, sentimental people expressing their feelings about this history, a part of which they proudly shared.

Columbus meant a great deal to them. His arrival was so real that they sang the story as though it had only just happened and they were telling us first-hand.

The next day was spent ashore visiting the people's homes. Many of these destitute people were ill. I took medicinal aids from our supply and did what I could for them. We hiked across the island about seven miles to the assumed spot where Columbus landed. At this remote location, a small sphere of marble representing the world had been set in a niche of a simple coral stone monument. A stone slab was inset in the coral and the inscription read: "On This Spot Christopher Columbus First Set Foot On The New World." It was here, perhaps, that he took possession of the island in the name of Spain, with due pomp and ceremony.

Since that first simple coral monument was placed on this bleak and barren shore in 1891, people who visualized other possible landing spots of Columbus and the crews of his fleet have added several other monuments. These people who came later questioned the decisions of the seafarers on board Columbus' boats. Surely, they thought, those sailors would not anchor on the reef on a windward shore in such shallow water. Such a tiny island—they would certainly sail around to a lee shore. Maybe not, for they were anxious to get ashore before they dropped off the edge of the world.

As I stood there by the simple coral stone marker, I did question that Columbus would anchor there where coral raised so near the surface of the sea.

It was exciting to stand there on the sugar sand beach and to feel the trade winds that had come across the expanse of sea from Spain along the same latitude known by *Niña*, *Pinta* and *Santa Maria*. I enjoyed imagining the world as it was and relive what I had read in my history books so many years before. It was a lonely scene as the sinking golden sun made long shadows beside the driftwood pieces along the beach and flashed brassy light through the curling surf that broke with a crash on the new world.

After a few days of enjoying this unusual habitation, we made our departure. I have found no finer sailing in the world than when moving on a beam reach in a balmy trade wind at maximum hull speed through the quiet water in the lee of low lying Fortune, Acklin, Mayaguana, Caicos and Great Inaqua Islands. It was a fantastic experience, for everything was right.

The wind funneled through Windward Passage at 20°10' North latitude and 74°00' West longitude between Cuba and the island of Haiti, giving us another fine sail to Navassa Island and on to Kingston, Jamaica, in the Caribbean.

Aids to navigation through the Bahamas and the Windward-Leeward Islands of the West Indies have been very wanting or even primitive for the more than 37 years I have made passages through them. The old British Admiralty charts dated in 1898 would indicate a possible light as an aid to navigation but a letter "U" would appear alongside the light, which in the legend would indicate this meant "unwatched." This intrigued me, so I went ashore at some of these designated lights and usually found crooked old driftwood posts about six feet high with a piece of scrap wood nailed on the top as a pedestal. On these scraps of wood, usually but not always, were old dilapidated kerosene lanterns. The native who lived in the lean-to shack on the beach nearest the post was supposed to light the lantern. If he forgot that evening or ran out of lantern oil— no aid to navigation! It made navigating all the more challenging.

To starboard was the east coast of Cuba where the Northeast trade winds found us and blew freshly. This was an historical setting made all the more interesting by passing the island with such a fine, solid wind. Cuba, the largest of the islands of the West Indies, approximately 760 miles in length, was all shades of green. Most impressively it rose out of the azure sea to mountain peaks well over a mile high. This was such a contrast to the low, sandy islands of the Bahamas. Cuba is a great sailing area with beautiful coves and harbors along her 2,000 miles of coastline. I look forward to the day when Castro, in friendship, will open her shores to us again. This great island was also discovered by Christopher Columbus on his first voyage from Spain in 1492, the same month he landed at Watling, San Salvador. He landed at the beautiful, almost landlocked, Bay of Nuevitas on the north coast, a short sail down from Acklin, the island we had just left. Of course, he also took it over in the name of the King of Spain.

In my many cruises throughout all of the West Indies, I observed a humorous aside. On practically every island, however remote, I noticed very large hand made iron anchors of the old kedge type. They were usually located in a native meeting place, in the shade of a tree or in the village square. They were painted shiny black or whitewashed, depending upon availability of the covering agent. The proud black natives of each island spoke of the anchor's history and would tell me his anchor was an anchor from Columbus' flagship. Columbus' little ship must have been heavily loaded with anchors.

Through the shrouds off *Tamarit's* port side we could see the colorful and majestic Dominican Republic. This tall island is one of the Greater Antilles group and lies between Cuba and Puerto Rico. From the middle of the Windward Passage, the part of the Dominican Republic we could see more in detail now was Haiti. The western portion of this big island was known as Hispaniola or "Little Spain." Haiti is very mountainous and heavily wooded and appeared velvety from our position offshore. To me, Haiti is one of the most captivating islands in our Western Hemisphere. It rises from tropical sea level heat and lush growth to 10,302 feet at Mount Tina where it is cold but cultivatable, thus permitting people to live at the altitude to which they best adapt. Their soils are very fertile but in need of revitalizing and while its inhabitants are mostly Negroes, there are great numbers of mulatto Haitians, the descendants of French settlers. French is the language of Haiti but the poor, uneducated Haitian tries to impress with French salutations and, running out of words, soon lapses off into a debased Creole patois, a native brew of language. Haiti is in the slow process of going from slavery to being recognized as a nation—very slowly.

I have sailed to Haiti several times and find it mysterious and extremely interesting. It is the land of the voodoo folk religion where special gods are invited to enter people's bodies in veiled secrecy, hence mystification, the hypnotic drums, sacrifices, bloodletting, and the quickly started, bombosh ceremonies. The beliefs, the superstitions, orgies, people possessed with the horse, donkey, pig, chicken, or whatever, and the animals that take the souls of the departed and live on with the living; fire walkers, wild dancers in unreal trances, the chants, the rhythms, cult practices with primitive African influences and so much of all this mixed with religion, alcohol, sex and poverty—all intensely serious for it is important to the millions who practice it. Many years ago and later during the repressive reign of the soft-spoken President for Life, Dr. Francois Duvalier, I sailed into the harbor of Port-au-Prince. I had set out from Connecticut skippering the 83' schooner *Queen Mab*, formerly owned by Harold Vanderbilt. The first leg in the Atlantic was to Bermuda, south to Fortune Island in the Bahamas and down the Windward Passage to Port-au-Prince. I spent over two months in Haiti cruising its coasts, enjoying every minute of the days and nights. There is no place in the world like it. Despite its charm, the nation struggles as one of the world's poorest.

The Haitians are to be admired for their indomitable spirit. Held down, repressed, enslaved, they have, as a nation and as individuals, had only one direction to go— up. They have been down, knocked back and smothered generation after generation. All they can do is rise; they can't go down for that is where they are. They find good in every defeat and cling to that good. Nothing is discarded; there is something useful in everything. I feel sorry for the 'boat people' of Haiti who escape and are returned, for they will have a long way to go back up to zero.

The average per capita income when I first sailed there many years ago was $60 a year. It is now $480 a year.[1] There are thousands and thousands who make nothing. It is hard to imagine such poverty. The ravages of malnutrition waste the people, the mortality rate is unbelievably high and disease has been rampant. Under former President Papa Doc, Françoise Duvalier, they have been a frightened people with the threat of flogging, imprisonment and murder. This "terror control" was carried out by Duvalier's "bogeymen," the tontoms macoute, something of a secret police. Fear was constantly in every home no matter how depressed and poor the occupants. Duvalier trusted no one and the people in town have come to trust no one. A "bogeyman" could be your neighbor. Many were taxi drivers. My first encounter was in the late 50's. I approached a so-called taxi man and asked to be taken to Petionville.

---

[1] As of 2003. Taken from World Bank Group.

By my attire and skipper's cap he didn't know what to do about my request. A quick look around him revealed a black man in a blue serge civilian suit. He was wearing dark glasses and a shirt open at the neck and chest. His coat bulged at the hip. My taxi man was noticeably frightened and in Creole began a rapid exchange of words with him. Finally the man in the suit approached, looking at me intently, and asked, "Why do you go to Petionville?"

I decided to banter him. I replied, "To find my friend."

He wagged a finger back and forth saying, "You cannot go."

I replied, "I want to go to Kenscoff."

He said, "No" with another finger wag.

I thought enough of this. I might get tossed in the prison—which happened very easily during that period. Duvalier had a full prison. I then continued, "I want this driver to take me to Villa Rosa. I have an audience in 10 minutes with Horace Ashton, the retired Cultural Attaché to the United States." Ashton's name was magic. It was the key to Haiti for me. He had been my host years before and when I phoned him as I came ashore that morning, he invited me to come to his Villa.

The "bogeyman" spoke rapidly in Creole to the driver to deliver me post haste to the Villa and bowed to me. He was immediately my friend.

Mr. Ashton spent most of his life in Haiti. He was the first white man to be permitted the 'unheard of' to photograph the secret voodoo ceremonies. He gave me a book, which was written in French, titled "Le Vodou Haitian" in which those photos were first to appear. He was a fascinating man, a storyteller equaled by Bing Crosby and Walter Cronkite who had the same ability to capture one's complete attention and hold it. Mr. Ashton was the Commodore of the Port-au-Prince Yacht Club. He owned a beautiful section of the beach at Arcachon where I had anchored with his permission. Speaking of a yacht club in this area of poverty, let me explain that at that time there was a well-to-do colony of 300 Caucasians, mostly Americans, accounting for the yacht club and possibly the four yachts. But Mr. Ashton knew boats and had sailed, thus he was a good Commodore and an aid to visiting boatmen. Ashton was well schooled and could talk on any subject—a worldly man who housed people in exile, from all parts of the world. It was interesting to sit in his big dining room, breaking bread with people of many nations—an unusual and valuable experience. Ashton sent his two sons to the United States to be educated but he stayed on in Haiti for there he was highly respected and lived in his Villa Rosa like a king. Mrs. Ashton was charming and to dine at her table with all its splendor and servants was remarkable.

The dictatorship by "Papa Doc" Duvalier and his family lasted twenty-eight years. His son, Jean-Claude "Baby Doc" Duvalier, fled the country in 1986. Jean-Bertrand Aristide had won the presidency in a landslide democratic election in 1990. He was deposed in a military coup in 1991, and then restored to power in 1994 by U.S. Troops. Aristide was re-elected in a vote marred by an opposition boycott and low turnout. Just prior to publishing this book, Jean-Bertrand Aristide was forced from power.

The women of Haiti wear cloth head coverings, usually wrap-arounds, but on Sunday, they wear wide-brimmed, hand woven, straw hats. If the wind comes up while wearing a wide brim, they are quick to solve the problem by picking up a large rock and placing it atop the hat. Everything in Haiti is carried on their heads so when it was important to wear that Sunday hat, hold it on with a rock. One day I saw a lady wearing her hat with a very old flat iron balanced up there on the straw. She was proud of her hat and the flat iron.

Walking along a remote jungle path one afternoon, I heard odd chanting and steady clacking sounds. Two men appeared in very ragged clothes bearing a small, rough mahogany casket on their heads. A tiny baby had died. The mother in rags was next in the procession wearing a black piece of cloth around her arm signifying a member of her family had died and she was in mourning. More family in the procession and then village friends followed. The people, perhaps 25 of them in single file, had rocks the size of baseballs, one in each hand and were hitting the stones together. That was the clacking sound I had heard—sounds to appease the spirits and arouse the possessed. They went to a small clearing in the jungle where a grave was dug. In addition to the clacking of stones there were people chanting while lying prostrate. The coffin was placed in the grave and covered. Other mounds were there but no markers were in evidence however, some were adorned with chicken feathers stuck in the soft earth.

One day I went to the Health Department to see if I could help alleviate some of the suffering I was seeing. So many children with thin arms and legs, with bloated, distended bellies, gaunt expressions and some too weak to walk. People with crooked legs with huge open sores that looked like compound fractures called yaws. People with noses gone, no legs, elephantiasis, and leprosy were most in evidence. I asked a Haitian doctor what was the cause. He told me, maybe to turn away the subject, that it was from walking in the tall grass. Others told me it was a type of venereal disease.

The poorer Haitians, being too destitute to buy food, had poor diets, which often produced undernourishment. As a result they suffered from chronic hookworm and malaria. Many Haitians have sore, infected eyes and many are blind. Tuberculosis was common and on the streets were many mental cases. The doctor at the Health Department took me aside. "Please," he said, "when you get to America, send medicines; perhaps you can find surplus medicine. Please send medicine!" This I arranged when I got back. They needed it then, they need it today.

Another insight to Haiti came unexpectedly one afternoon as I stood on the beach of a small, remote village. A crowd gathered at the water's edge. Not knowing why and being 300 yards away, I started taking pictures as I hurried over hoping to get a sequence of whatever was happening. Two black Haitian policemen in their khaki uniforms and caps were leading a tall, square shouldered black man down to the water's edge. The black man's wrists were tied together at his back and another sisal line cinched his elbows together uncomfortably tight at the small of his back. The man was in rags, barefooted, barelegged with torn old patched shorts and tattered shirt. His head was hairless, black and shining. He was very tall, muscled and thin. He was impressive. A lady was frantically hanging on to him and pleading with the officers in French Creole. She was dressed in black with a black hat and was barefooted. I learned from an English speaking Haitian standing near the scene that she was the wife of the prisoner.

A large skiff was anchored out just past the surf line. In its bow rode a flagstaff flying the flag of Haiti. On shore, a short, stocky, barefooted Haitian stepped quickly behind the prisoner, stooped down, placed his head between the prisoner's legs. Rising up, he lifted the prisoner onto his shoulders. He carried the prisoner through the surf to the skiff and deposited him on the thwart amidships. The short man came back and carried the policeman to the skiff in the same manner. He returned, lifted the prisoner's wife the same way and placed her in the bow thwart. The policeman pulled in the anchor, started the motor and departed straight out to sea.

To the Haitian standing beside me I said, "What is this about?"

In a sad voice he answered, "The prisoner has just killed a black man. He will be taken seven miles out in the ocean with his arms and hands bound, he will be allowed to stand up and jump overboard. If he cannot jump, the policeman will throw him over. His wife is there to witness his fate."

"There are big sharks out there," I replied, "I have seen them."

He explained that if the prisoner can survive, if the sharks spare him, if he can swim with his arms tied, he would be free.

"Is this sentence the decision of the court?"

"No, the policeman makes the decision after he talks to those involved. It is quick."

No representation, no jury, hearsay considered, decision. To me this was a poor Haitian again having hit bottom. There was no place to go but up. By the look on that prisoner's face, he would fight to go up. Somehow, I felt he would gain his freedom. One day I will return and someone, perhaps his wife, will tell me he made it. Maybe I will meet the man himself. I'll know him by his stature and the expression on his face, the set of his jaw—up!

The sea, the sky and the warm semitropical trade winds were incentive to raise the anchor so that *Tamarit* could take us to another new world.

Ahead of us on the starboard bow, the horizon was unrolling another scenic discovery made by Columbus—the lofty island of Jamaica, formerly known as Xaymaca. He didn't get to this island until his second trip back from Spain in 1494. Here, also, he found Arawak Indians for they had been here since A.D. 750. A Spanish colony was created in Jamaica in 1509.

England sent out an expedition under Oliver Cromwell to capture Hispaniola, the island from which we had just cruised. That attempt failed, so the force sailed the approximate same course we were now holding with *Tamarit* and landed on this island of Jamaica. They were successful in killing most of the Spaniards and drove the remaining Spanish guerillas into the mountains where they held out for five years until 1660. The Spanish had previously brought in African slaves to do their labor. With the Spanish defeated, the slaves, left ashore some time ago to their fate under the desolate conditions of survival, sought refuge in the mountain vastness and formed the nucleus of the Maroons. These fugitive, rebellious slaves brought forth a people that are proud, that have risen from zero to become an island nation of approximately 2,000,000-plus people. Slavery begun was difficult to eradicate. It spread throughout the West Indies and to our colonies. Thomas Jefferson once said, "The abolition of domestic slavery is the greatest object of desire in these colonies, where it was unhappily introduced in their infant state."

Selfish, unthinking people nurtured the problems of slavery. It brought disgrace to so many. The British Parliament abolished slave trade in 1807 between Africa and Jamaica.

When I look at these black people I see that as Typius Maximus said, "No one is a slave whose will is free." They are on their way up—masters of their fates. Each generation away from the stigma is rising. They will make it, for as a native once said, "We feel that there is no color barrier—we enjoy the white people. The piano has black and white keys, played together great music and harmony comes forth. There is room for all in God's world."

It was a dramatic sail from Watling Island (San Salvador) down past these colorful islands that have had, and continue to have, so much to do with the New World's history. As we approached Morant Point on the east end of Jamaica, the beautiful green tropical island's high, blue mountain peak rose to over 7,400 feet above the sea. It was sundown and we were tossing beautiful sparkling spray as we scudded into another beautiful picture. *Tamarit* was alive and driving toward this island of wonderful velvety colors. Sailing close to the shore we could see the flowering shrubs of brilliant scarlet, yellow, white and great masses of variegated, rich green trees. There were waterfalls and breaking surf along the rocky shore. The name Jamaica is an Arawak Indian word meaning the Isle of Springs called the Queen of the Caribbean.

The trade winds were pungently filled with spicy fragrance from the blooms of the pimiento allspice tree. Spoondrift from the sea's crests and this fragrance blended with a never-to-be-forgotten sunset. This is the type of memory to which the boatman clings. A scent of blooms mixed with sea spray years from now will transport me to relive those moments at the helm of a schooner in tune with her element, driving and alive with a necklace of bubbling foam, sparkling white, on an azure sea. It was all there to make for great moments.

In a setting like this, I thought of Sir Henry Morgan, the great dashing pirate-buccaneer who for so long made Port Royal, of this massive island, his headquarters. He made Port Royal famous and it became one of the richest places in the world.

Sir Henry led his buccaneers across the isthmus at Panama, and sacked and burned Old Panama City in 1671. He left the city ruined. It never recovered. He took mule loads of treasure back to Port Royal. Three years later, the new City of Panama, the present capital, sprang up 5 miles away at a better location. The buccaneers brought their loot from their plundering of Spanish territories to Port Royal and here the desperadoes squandered the riches they had stolen. Port Royal was a place that gloried in its reputation developed from stolen wealth and wickedness. It came to a sudden end, however, for on a hot afternoon there was an odd sound like the wind of a squall whistling, followed by a roar. Then came a terrorizing rumble like the mountains were coming down in an avalanche. The ground heaved and rocked violently. People were thrown to the ground. Houses were laid flat and the thunderous crashes sent up clouds of black dust which hung over the island for days. Fires completed the destruction. Port Royal was finished!

Survivors founded the new city of Kingston. It was more substantially built but not enough so, for in 1907, another terrible earthquake devastated Kingston. This city is also often subjected to hurricanes and must keep alert during the hurricane season.

Around the end of the island on the south shore was the harbor of Kingston, our destination. The crew was anxious for another island adventure and a chance to try their legs on land. Mr. Henry Tenny suggested, since dark was upon us, that we hold our course on past the island for 60 miles and wait until dawn to sail in. I reasoned with him that we would have to beat back against the heavy seas and trade winds, and we wouldn't get into Kingston until the next evening. He thought it was dangerous to sail the Jamaica coast at night and with no moon. I told him I would have the *Tamarit* lying off the entrance to Kingston Harbor at the break of dawn and save a day. He was skeptical but I was ready. All night I stayed at the helm and as the dawn broke, there was Kingston and the pungent odor wafted out to us was from the Myer's Rum distillery near the waterfront.

We had arrived at this fascinating land of places like Port Antonio, Montego Bay, Ocho Rios, and Manchioneal. Jamaica is peopled by African descendents, by Maroons, a nation to themselves. They are mixtures of East Indian, Welsh, French, English, and Chinese, and now, in later years, by the controversial sect that worships Ethiopia's Haile Selassie, who, though deceased, still lives for these people. He is their God and they have taken his given name of Ras Tafari, the name he carried before being made King of Ethiopia, and call themselves Rastafarians. They were readily recognized by their wild hairdos of wiry strands twisted together, dyed or colored. We found them easygoing, mild and peace loving in spite of their almost threatening appearance. Birth control has not been practiced very much in Jamaica—perhaps the opposite has been encouraged. Excessive amounts of marijuana are smoked by some of the natives.

Up went the British Merchant flag at our starboard spreader and beneath it the yellow quarantine flag. We tacked in, timing our approach to not be in the quarantine area before 0800 to avoid an overtime charge by the Customs and Immigration officials.

We were cleared and proceeded under sail to the Royal Jamaica Yacht Club where my Transpacific Yacht Club membership card was recognized. Guest privileges and Jamaican hospitality were a beautiful combination we began to enjoy.

It was Saturday and word got about that an American yacht was at the Yacht Club. That was reason for a cocktail party and *Tamarit's* crew was given a "Hip, Hip" British welcome. A sea-walled basin was adjacent to the Yacht Club and the Commodore asked that I anchor the schooner in the middle of the basin so she could swing.

"She is so beautiful we want to look at her from the club's salon and veranda. Besides," he said, "it is time for 'serious drinking,' whatever that is."

I was quite tired from being up two days and a night but *Tamarit* was anchored and cleaned up. This gave me new life. Besides, the odor of rum was heavy on the air. Bob had handled the anchor and had given me the scope of chain length I had indicated. He thought he had properly set the pawl on the windlass wildcat to hold the chain, but . . .

We went ashore to meet with the assembled yachtsmen and dignitaries. Rum did flow. Fortunately, hors d'oeuvres were readily available to counter the many toasts as the toaster was really smoking hot. Well into the joviality and tinkle of glasses, a sudden violent squall bent the palms like hunting bows and blew napkins and tablecloths askew on the veranda, and waitresses ran to retrieve them. The wind whistled! I was chatting with the club officers and looked beyond them at *Tamarit*. She was swinging violently to the wind but didn't right herself. I heard and recognized the awful sound of chain rattling out of the hause pipe. I called to Bob to come quickly, left my drink, excused myself to our hosts with a shout and tore out of the club. Bob was at the dory at the same time I arrived. Painter off the dock cleat, oarlocks in place, we shoved off and I pulled oars like never before. With the wind helping, we scooted, a bone in her teeth. Over my shoulder, as I bent the oars, I could see *Tamarit* was running her chain out fast. She was on her way to the sea wall. Bringing the dory to the boarding ladder, I clambered to the deck as Bob secured the dory's painter. I ran to the windlass and jammed my foot on the chain to slow it up as it was singing and clattering up out of the chain locker, nearly losing my shoe and the starboard foot to the violently flying links. Bob arrived on the foredeck and as the chain slowed, he flipped the pawl in place on the teeth of the wildcat, stopping the chain. Needless to say, adrenalin was flowing. *Tamarit* responded and came up sharply, stopped by her anchor and chain. *Tamarit*'s teak taffrail and transom were close enough to the sea wall that, had we wished to do so, we could have stepped off the deck onto the wall. Another whew!! I started the diesel to heave ahead. Bob brought in the chain with the windlass and we returned to the original anchored location. Bob was careful this time to heave and pawl the windlass. We tied the pawl down this time with some ratline stuff and went back to retrieve our rum. Another toast to Bob and me with "Hip! Hip! Hooray! Good show you blokes! Bloody good show!" Great hospitality was had at the Royal Jamaica Yacht Club and another burgee for my collection.

We went to dinner that evening at the hotel. There is something British about the British for we couldn't dine unless we wore ties and white cotton starched (awful) dinner jackets over our sailing T-shirts. The garments were provided in the lobby, they didn't fit and looked like hell but we were legal. *Tamarit* sat still that night as at last we slept.

A place I wanted to visit in Jamaica was Shaw Park Manor. To go there it was necessary to be scrutinized closely and cleared at the agency desk in Kingston. The reason for this caution was that this fine resort some 30 miles up in the mountains served dinner by reservations only and the guests used solid silver service. They would like to retain this expensive table silver. The Commodore of the Yacht Club vouched for us. The drive up to the Manor was like a color moving picture that kept unfolding beauty, scenes, people doing everything and animals completing the panorama. We left the heat as we rose into the mountains and rain forests. A fertile island blessed with subterranean waters had brought forth heavy, lush growth. Spices, bananas, figs, sweet potatoes, plantains, cassavas, wild yams, chocho squash, sugarcane, coffee, tobacco, coconuts, citrus, mangoes, pineapple, rice, and more, and there with it all, the odor of molasses and rum.

Shaw Park Manor was worth the whole sailing trip. A beautiful masonry gate and winding wall led to a promontory over which flew the colorful flags of the Caribbean Islands. The lodge was of matching masonry like the wall and gate. The bar, also of select stonework, had windows made from the bottoms of colorful wine and rum bottles through which shone the tropical sun, giving interesting color and light effects. The feature of the formal estate, with its flowers and manicured lawns, was the languid river and waterfalls that made their way through the three beautifully shaped, tile swimming pools set on three different levels. This river kept the pools constantly fresh and cool.

Torrid nightlife and fascinating day life made it difficult for us to sail away but after ten days, we set a definite departure time. We obtained clearance papers, replenished provisions, water and fuel. The akee, the national fruit, a full stem of bananas and coconuts were but a portion of the fresh fruit. It was mango, custard apple and pineapple time so we filled the dory, keeping it on deck, handy for our taste buds.

We bid our yacht club friends farewell, sailed out to the outer harbor, entered the main channel and as we approached the last channel marker, a huge cruise ship out of Sweden pulled alongside on our course. The passengers were in a festive mood and gathered on the rails above us. We exchanged bantered joviality. Someone called down, "Where are you bound?"

I called back, "Panama!"

Someone said, "So are we. We will race you there!"

"Great," I called back, "let's go!" For I love a race and with a twin-screw ship that was going to make it sporting—with *Tamarit* under sail.

Our challenging friends yelled out merry encouragement and immediately I asked Bob to break out the big #1 170% genoa jib and the fisherman. We trimmed the sails and moved a few yards to weather (away from the ship) then settled down to make her go. *Tamarit* was on a reach with the wind three degrees forward of the beam. On port tack, she started to move out making knots down to Panama—600 miles away. The seas were big rollers and the troughs were deep canyons. *Tamarit* scooted down parallel with the troughs and with her high freeboard, she rose to scoot parallel to the crests, throwing the foam into beautiful fury. It was like she was built for this. She gained her hull speed and she hummed, leaving the lovely mountainous isle astern, sinking in the white-capped sea. We felt sorry for the big rolling cruise ship for under these conditions, she had to alter course, reaching off for the easiest ride. *Tamarit's* sails kept us from rolling. The little David and the big Swedish Goliath were off for Panama across the Spanish Main to the land of Balboa.

Tamarit under sail. *Photo by Jim Delorey.*

One of the finest sails I have ever experienced for six hundred miles in less than three days brought us to Panama Harbor around the breakwater abeam the cruise ship, our bows right together. A great finish with horns blaring. It was exciting. We received our Panamanian Customs clearance, a pilot was assigned for the Canal transit and orders came to move into the first lock with the Swedish ship. The passengers lowered three bottles of champagne to us to commemorate our thrilling race.

We began our transit through the Panama Canal's first lock, later to be lifted in three lifts eighty-five feet to the elevation of Gatun Lake. As we entered this first lock and the gates closed behind us, I said to Bob, "You know Richard Halliburton wrote in his book, 'Royal Road to Romance,' that he swam through these Panama locks."

Bob said, "Yeh?!"

So over we dove, not to be outdone by Richard—and that was a mistake! We had no sooner hit the water than we realized it to be so. Sewage and some garbage coming through the pumps from the ships' galleys attract sharks and this was no exception. Fins were moving about us. Bob and I saw them at the same time. What a scramble we made getting back on *Tamarit's* deck. Whew! Our pilot was quite amused. A White Death Shark in the Gulf Stream had bumped me, and that was enough!

Richard Halliburton also told in his book of swimming the length of the reflecting pool in front of the Taj Mahal at Agra, India. When there at this remarkable place, I stuck my index finger in the pool to the knuckle and the depth of the water was the length of my finger—three and three quarter inches. It is a long pool, possibly 100 meters, so Richard must have had badly bruised elbows and knees—and could have scraped his keel!

Al Adams in front of the *Taj Mahal* at Agra, India
Photo taken by Dianne H. Adams

In my travels, I met David Wynn, the King of Vagabonds. I wrote a published story about his travels. He gave me a picture he had taken of himself standing in the middle of the Taj's sacred reflecting pool. The water's surface was to his ankles—three and three-quarter inches deep. Richard's was a good story, anyway.

The Panama Canal never ceases to be fascinating. It has reality and distinctiveness—there is nothing like it in the world. The French started the preparation of cutting through the Continental Divide to build the Canal in 1880, but mismanagement, disease, mud and so much more defeated them. It was estimated 20,000 deaths resulted. The French effort cost more than a billion francs and nine years of struggle. Malaria's wracking "shakes" was a threat to all, but yellow fever, known as "black vomit," was deadly. It could kill a person in twenty-four hours. Had it not been for Col. William C. Gorgas' efforts in those early days, we probably would not have the Canal to give away, for he paved the way by stopping the yellow fever and the malaria problem. The French cemetery outside Panama City gives silent evidence of the lost lives.

United States General Goethals was the man who completed the mind boggling engineering feat and great credit is due all the men who carried out the detailed orders to make it a reality.

So many Americans lost their lives here. It was impressive to sail through and fanaticize. As we sailed through the vast project, I was impressed with the bronze plaques set in the solid rock cliff faces commemorating our men who died in this endeavor. To think that 200 million cubic yards of rock and dirt was excavated for the Canal. Some of the banks are being excavated to widen them further from 300 to 500 feet. The lock chambers were built 1,000 feet long and 110 feet wide. They were opened for travel in 1914, and all vessels built up to that year could transit. The largest ice-breaking ship ever built is 1,005 feet long, so, by her length alone, she could not transit. In the 1930's, ships were being built which could not enter the locks. The great ship *Queen Mary* had to go around Cape Horn. My wife and I made the last great cruise on the *Queen Mary* to Long Beach, California. A trip of a lifetime—and on her around Cape Horn, South America. In the locks we watched one U.S. aircraft carrier move through with only 7 inches of clearance. The ship carried a list angle pre-calculated to clear the ship's projections. Also, thought was given in the Canal's design stage so that the Control Building adjacent to the locks could drop its eaves for ship clearance. A big ship with little clearance has to be pulled or driven into the locks. The ship's displacement creates pressure, which unless overcome, will push her back out of the tight locks, an unbelievable force.

From my previous trips through the Canal, I was aware of the necessity for conversing with the control station operator prior to entering the locks. He wanted every vessel to have long dock and spring lines ready before the vessel went into the locks. The lines should be secured to strong cleats on the vessel's decks. Those lines, when pulled up later to the tops of the locks by the professional line heavers, would have to reach up approximately 75 feet. Before we could begin transiting the locks, our lines were inspected. If the lines were not adequate, one was told where to go to buy adequate lines. The control man asked if I wanted a side-tie or to ride on-center in the locks. I wanted the center of the locks position because the lock gates close and water rushes in from the sides below the waterline. This water serves to float the vessels up 85 feet in three lifts. The water rushes in with great force. If it comes in from one side stronger or sooner than the other side, the force hits the boat's keel, pushing the hull laterally. If the vessel is close to the massive stone sides, the masts' spreaders could hit the masonry and break. The masts could fall if the shrouds go loose with broken spreaders.

The Canal operates day and night. Today it handles approximately 26,000 ships a year and anticipates another

1,000 by 2005. It takes about nine hours for the average vessel to transit the Canal and Gatun Lake. A ship's owner pays to transit the Canal primarily on the basis of tonnage. At the time of the *Tamarit* delivery large ships could pay perhaps $20,000 or more. The owners are happy to do so for without the Canal they would have to go around South America by way of Cape Horn. That could cost roughly $50,000 in lost time and expense. I transited with my 40-foot cutter one trip. The charge was $26.00 and that included the pilot for nine hours. Inflation has now sailed into the Zone.

We enjoyed conversing with our pilot. He was informative; he liked *Tamarit*, our food and drink. It was good contrast for him to be on a yacht instead of a big ore ship, a tugboat, a tanker, a cruise ship or a barge. He told us that huge tankers coming through will need four pilots: two on the bridge, one to port and one to starboard, and two way aft, one to port and one to starboard. There are a goodly number of collisions in the narrow cuts and curving channels.

When the Canal was begun, it was necessary to build the Gatun Dam to back up and create a Gatun Lake with water area of 163 square miles. Then the mind boggler, to me, watching all the happenings as *Tamarit* pulled out onto this huge lake, is the fact that this big operation is not possible without fresh water from the rainfall. Without the normal rainfall, the Canal could not function, for it takes 52 million gallons of fresh water for each ship that transits and on the average, forty ships go through each day. The Chagres River fed by Panama's heavy rains supplies this water.

Gatun Lake is interesting and ghostly for dead trees stick up from the bottom in grotesque shapes. It was tempting to us to leave the marked channel and explore but we had a pilot to think about. We saw howling monkeys, beautifully plumed parrots, and orchids. Occasionally, a snake was in evidence. In the jungles, out of view, were jaguars, three-toed sloth and the dread poisonous Fer de Lance snakes, similar to the rattlesnake but without rattles.

We dined under *Tamarit's* awning as we cruised along with the yacht's diesel humming. We met ships and boats, tugs and barges, ships from Germany, Italy, and Norway, and United Fruit Company's fast banana boats. It was exciting to enter the first lock on the Atlantic side, then the second, then the third, and then the fourth to be lowered 85 feet to the level of the Pacific Ocean. It was surprising, too, to look up and see a huge ship in the adjacent locks 85 feet above us going to the Atlantic. We bid our pilot farewell. He had changed from his sun togs back into his business suit ready to start back for Cristobal and still another assignment to transit the Canal.

As we powered over to the Balboa Yacht Club, I was studying the overall chart of Panama and its surrounding islands. This would be a wonderful area to spend a few years just cruising, for there are 609 islands on the Caribbean side and 1011 on the Pacific side. That would be a great adventure and good anchoring practice. The sea and islands continue to strongly attract my human spirit—to find adventure and to seek and to satisfy basic curiosities about myself as well as about nature. Thinking about the West Indies and all that has gone before, I determined that the sea has been exciting and useful to man, helping him to set foot on its many and varied shores. My great fascination for islands is only kindled the more as I think on the other islands of the world rising out of the sea that, as yet, I haven't brought up on those far horizons.

We registered at the desk of the Balboa Yacht Club and were assigned a mooring. I made a quick schedule of work assignments for each one of us and we followed this work with welcome shower baths at the Club. At the dock we then took on fresh water, provisions and diesel fuel. We turned in.

The first part of the night brought rain pelting the cabin top cooling the night air and lulling us into euphoria. The last of the rain made gurgling and soothing sounds as it made its way from the deck and cabin top down through the scuppers. The night grew quiet and *Tamarit* slept!

The Pacific lay restless but peaceful, beckoning to us to come out beyond the Gulf of Panama. We had traveled the East Coast's inland waterway, we had sampled the Atlantic Ocean, we had enjoyed the alluring Caribbean, and now *Tamarit* was pointed toward the Pacific, another home of the King of the Sea with his whiskers of seaweed, his trident and his dolphins beckoning—anxious to share adventure.

We now had 2,850 miles to go to Tamarit's new home, the impressive harbor of San Diego, California. Many weeks of sailing lay ahead, most of it close hauled, every mile to be earned. A lot of waves to be plowed through and so many more fascinating lands of Middle America to feel *Tamarit*'s bow wave.

Oddly, we had to sail south before we could sail north toward California to get around the Peninsula De Azuero. Then we began the trek along Panama's Pacific side. Costa Rica, sometimes called the Switzerland of Middle America, was next. Columbus was here also (on the Caribbean side) and when he arrived he saw Indians wearing gold ornaments and named the country Costa Rica—Rich Coast. That was in 1502.

The land strip is narrow here. Narrow as Panama at the Canal. Most of Costa Rica is the mountainous backbone of the Continental Divide that on the way up north, becomes the Rocky Mountains and on south becomes the Andes. Costa Rica straddles that range that separates the Pacific Ocean from the Caribbean. From the deck the scenes were impressive as we anchored in close to the sandy beaches crowded with lush jungle growth. Natives could be seen with their primitive two-wheeled carts being drawn by oxen. Naked children played in the surf. From the sea level our eyes lifted with the sharp climb to Costa Rica's rugged ranges that include active volcanoes. I thought of Mt. Fuji of Japan with the sight of those volcanic cones as we cove-hopped along.

I have long been fascinated with Costa Rica. It has a bewildering range of climate from warm, rainy jungle, cloud-bathed forests and even desert-like plateaus on up to those piercing 11,000-foot volcanic peaks that stab the cloud-patched sky. This dramatic little country, famous for coffee and bananas, has an extraordinarily rich variety of birds, reptiles, and monkeys. We found wild hogs that were wonderful to roast on the beach while *Tamarit* waited at anchor.

In the higher altitudes we found grass-covered areas called savannahs where the Ricans had fincas and stock farms, raising cattle and a great breed of horses. Rain forests brought many surprises, so many species of life. We were intrigued with high, shrill, piercing sounds which turned out to be frogs—limitless frogs. When it rained, they were obvious and noisy—a din that was overwhelming. Checking closer, I found it was the males that made the music; it was their operatic love song. It got me and surely it got them mates. These frogs, like none I had ever seen, were many colored and brilliant. Some were chameleon-like, remarkable for the changes of color of their skin according to their surroundings, sunlight changes, or, I imagined, the sensual mood they were in. It could be that a "fickle frog" is more colorful, also more demonstrative. For certain they seemed noisier. Their tones and passages to my un-frogged ear were sung forte.

There were frogs of many sizes but most were of such size they would be content to sit on a postage stamp. In Hawaii I had found "fragile frogs" so transparent, the entire skeletal frame was obvious. In Jamaica, I had heard frogs that were so shrill, and trilled in such high key, that they were difficult to find. They would extend their throats to a length longer than their bodies. A male frog in Peru carries its young on its back until the young feels it can make it on its own. Female frogs, of some species, carry their eggs under their skin on their backs, looking very lumpy, until the eggs are nudged into position to hatch. This reminded me of those olive green toads in Chile up to 12 inches in length whose meat, warts and all, tastes similar to a cross between chicken and Nantucket lobster.

I had to caution the crew about two things as we trekked over the terrain, into the gorges, the sides of the volcanoes and along streams into the rain forests—beware of snakes such as the Fer de Lance, Bushmasters, Rattlers and large Boas; and don't handle the "flirtive frogs" if you have open cuts on your hands. Some of those highly attractive dendrobatid frogs secrete a toxic poison, one of the most deadly known. It affects the nerves of birds and animals they contact. It will cause paralysis and kills quickly, so let their pretty colors be a warning.

The early primitive pre-Columbians were aware of this poison and utilized it. They would heat the bodies of the frogs, causing the skin to give off the poisonous mucous. This was smeared on their spear points, arrows and darts which they found most effective in war, and in peace on the hunts. In Hawaii, I found that if a dog, while playing with a Bufo frog, bit down, an excretion from nodules on its head would emit a mucous that would put the dog to sleep. Some frogs on the Dark Continent of Africa exceeded 30 inches in length. They would tip the scales at 7 pounds. In Mexico, at Puerto Vallarta, they were 10 inches across at the greatest girth.

Costa Rica is a wealthy country. It has had its up-swings and downers. Many Americans have settled there, many have plantations. Negroes and Spaniards have developed a nation of small farms, developed rich culture, political stability and a fairly high standard of living.

We sailed into the Gulfo Dulce to the harbor of Golfito where United Fruit loaded bananas on the beautiful, fast, twin-screw banana ships. A well-organized company, it had the banana business developed to a science. Years before, I made a trip from Panama to Golfito on the *Parismina*, a 34 knot, twin screw banana ship with the natives working all night loading the conveyor belts. The ship took on bananas twice prewashed and cellophane covered. We took off for San Francisco. The main office in the United States was in touch with the ship's captain at sea and they kept him posted on the market so that the captain could arrive at the unloading terminal in San Francisco when the market price for bananas was going to be advantageous. By slowing the ship's speed, or turning out a few more knots, the timing can pay off. Such a science it has become that the fruit is kept at the right temperature at sea and as the ship approaches the destination for unloading, the bananas can be brought to the temperature at the terminal.

Twin Screw Banana Ship *Parismina*
Photo taken by Al Adams, Skipper

Twin Screw Banana Ship *Parismina*
16 mm photos taken by Al Adams

Bananas in great quantities, in a ship's hold between decks, can give off a dangerous gas which can overcome a person who breathes it. On banana ships, blatant signs are posted near exhausting air ducts leading from the fruit in the hold warning people not to stand close. So well handled were the bananas, in passage, that the company and the ship's crew could boast that not one stem of banana was damaged out of all those tons of fruit.

Anchored in Gulfo Dulce harbor of Golfito, *Tamarit* was colorful with three beautiful tree-ripened stems of Costa Rican bananas hanging from her boom gallows. Until I had eaten a banana, ripe and ready, fresh off the tree, I didn't really know the delicious flavor of a banana. We had bananas every way. On boats in the tropics it is almost a standard routine that stems of bananas are taken on board. They often ripen too fast and it is discouraging to see them wasted. On *Tamarit* we peeled the ripe bananas, pureed them with a food mill, added the juice of a lemon or lime and kept it very cold. When we served banana daiquiris, even weeks later, it was delectable. The girls made banana bread, fried bananas, banana bars, banana plate compote, banana whip with orange cream, banana cake, banana pies, bananas and cereal, and their banana ice cream was great underway. The banana is really a rather recent development of several varieties and has been grown to last and mature while in transit. I like the banana best when the skin is quite yellow and very speckled, when the fruit is just soft. It peaks at its finest flavor and is delicious when it acquires this peak on the tree. Red or claret bananas are even more rich and sweet and little finger bananas are exceptional. I found, also, on the boat, that bananas baked in their jackets for about 25 minutes, split open, sprinkled with sugar and a touch of ignited rum served flaming, goes well when anchored in a moon-bathed tropical cove to the lift and scend of a quiet sea. They go well with baked albacore and linguini or tuna and Maine lobster, but especially well with crab legs, lime juice and melted butter. French bread and a variety of cheeses from Holland or Martinique served with the right wine is complementary to the versatile banana.

Morning dishes washed and stowed, we brought in the Herreshoff kedge anchor, our good old standby on any bottom. We made sail and sailed off the anchor then close reached out to Metalpo Point, hardened in on the sails and stood out to sea for ten miles. We brought her about and on port tack, beat up the Costa Rican coast past a point whose name always intrigues me—Sal-si-puedes, which means 'come out if you can.' Perhaps I will name my next boat Sal-si-puedes.

It was a glorious sail from anchor to anchor, 155 miles to an unbelievable little cove called Ballena Bay. A river emptied, fresh and slow, under gently swaying palm trees. Throwing the lead and line, I brought *Tamarit* well up into the fresh water where the soft flow held her steady. It was such a pleasant setting and this was one time I could climb the ratlines and pick coconuts without going ashore. Mahogany trees were the backdrops to our fabulous picture. Chattering monkeys swung wildly from the vines and flocks of parrots sent flashes of their color above the masts. It was a dream spot—a place that brought our little faraway world to its peak of meaning. *Tamarit*, as usual, was in tune with nature from anchor to anchor, and from sea to shining sea, she had served us well. With ample fresh water alongside, we washed away her salt crystals and chamoised her fresh and sparkling. Out in the bay, intriguing black and brown rock stacks and little islets with lush tropical growth on their tops, like ladies' hats, partially blocked the entrance where they rose out of the sea. They guarded the entrance to this mariner's haven and quieted the surf before letting it in so not to disturb a sailor's heaven.

It was difficult to depart this private little world. Any other nationality would no doubt have stayed there. Americans are on schedule. They don't relax in paradise. They stand watches and if some crewman is five minutes late coming on watch, they get upset. I like the well-run yacht, and with Americans, it seems to be vital to be on time but its fun to sail with the Polynesians, for schedules don't mean much. The next man on watch may be playing his guitar. He may never come on watch—nobody cares.

Tamarit was always ready for sea. She had a great feeling helm. She was powerful, a well-balanced schooner. I liked her husky masts and heavy standing rigging. There was not a sound in her hull beating to weather. Everything about her was right for the next sea encounter. She had a way with the sea.

I have sailed from Cape Horn to the Bering Sea and it is usual to enjoy the sail from north to south, but I enjoy the south to north cruise the best. The tendency is to miss so much when sailing free. Making good time, one tends to pass up the great coves. Going north, slogging to weather, having a good day or two of northing and then putting in to enjoy the land, the people and the off-the-beaten-path adventure. Adventure is found in places one can seldom get to unless by a small boat, where ships and planes cannot reach. Small vessels are seclusion finders.

The numbers of people who have been to more islands than I are few. Islands, to me, are fascinating. They are places of the unusual because they are usually remote and remote makes for the remarkable, the unique and the rare.

Columbus touched in at the eastern coast of what was to become Nicaragua. He had sailed through the cays and reefs of the Caribbean approach to Nicaragua's most easterly shore with a great shoal area and in a very bad storm. With charts and sailing directions not yet available, I don't understand how he made it. With good seamanship, he got in behind the point of land and weathered the storm. He was so relieved to have made it safely to anchor, having escaped the gale, that he named its north-eastern corner Cabo Gracias a Dios (Cape Thank God); Columbus was inspired, a devout man and I think he felt guided by God.

On the *Tamarit*'s bowsprit I stood watching Nicaragua attach itself to Costa Rica's mountain ranges, and rise high to take its place in the sun. We watched our geography from the deck as our panorama changed sailing north. For 270 miles we would see Nicaragua's coastline and her volcanic peaks, a fascinating, colorful part of the Andes range.

Nicaragua is the largest of the Central American Republics. It is the least densely populated of the Middle American countries. We found much heavy rain in the jungles to the east, while the western area is dotted with lakes and volcanoes. The central area is high and mountainous. Most of the people seemed to prefer living in the steamy Pacific lowlands.

As we rounded Cabo Velas (Cape of Winds), it lived up to its name. It lies adjacent to the Gulf of Papagayo, where the dreaded Papagayo winds come screaming from offshore. We reefed down to be ready. Under just-reefed staysail and reefed foresail, we scudded along on a beam reach, enjoying the sail and the scenes of the land. *Tamarit* sailed close to converge with the mahogany covered land. The closer to shore, the smoother the seas. As the wind increased, we lowered the jib. The water was deep up to the shore. Under the foresail alone, we brought her in and dropped the anchor off San Juan Del Sur. The wind blew hard, but it was pleasant, with streaks of hot land air mixed with cool, for just a short distance inland was Lake Nicaragua. The wind coming from over the lake was pleasant. Strong as the wind was, there was no sea running under the land and *Tamarit* pointed her bowsprit toward the wind and the land. It was a choice situation. Out at sea it would have been a wet ride. This was nice for the evening and a night's sleep.

Lake Nicaragua is 96 miles long and 39 miles wide, just north of it and connected by a shallow river named Tipitapa is Lake Managua, which is 38 miles long by 16 miles wide.

Lake Nicaragua was once a bay of the Pacific. It is one of the world's few fresh water lakes containing sawfish and man-eating sharks. In recent political uprisings, people rebelling against the ruling group were reportedly disposed of in the lake.

Just a mile offshore as we headed to anchor, Bob had brought in a fighting Dorado fish on the troll line. It was a beauty measuring 44 inches in length. Such a handsome creature in its brilliance of colors, then it succumbed to slate gray before our eyes. The girls baked it, and with limejuice, melted butter, baked yams, complemented with banana daiquiris, we enjoyed our new place in the world.

Columbus' world was behind us now, for history and his logbook brought evidence of his presence only as far as Nicaragua. To appreciate Columbus for the way he changed our world is one thing, to appreciate him for his indomitable courage was another. For if he had nothing else, to me, he was great, the way he would not be subdued. My appreciation goes much further—his seamanship, his navigation, his leadership with odds constantly against all three, deserves much praise. He made his charts as he went. He had no satellite navigation computer. He had no printed sailing directions. He had no digital Fathometer. He had neither a Plathe sextant nor the latest Hydrographic Office Method for celestial navigation. He had no latest Almanac. He had no quartz timepiece to give him Greenwich time. He had no life raft, no life jackets, no radar, no wind/speed instruments and no water maker. He had no engine but with all these "had nots," he had courage and common sense. He knew how to sail those small, poorly rigged vessels loaded with disbelieving crews— and of course, loaded to the gunnels with anchors (one for each island). He died a sick and beaten man, discredited in his own country, and in Spain, scorned and ignored. It seems he was a man on earth for a purpose too great for the average man to comprehend. Late as it was, he was ahead of his time. A philosopher wrote 1400 years before Columbus, "An age will come after many years when the ocean will loose the chains of things, and a huge land lie revealed." The amazing Columbus fulfilled that prophecy in 1492.

I have sailed to every place in the Caribbean that has been indicated and many more. That is why I have great respect for his accomplishment. As I approached each landfall, I thought of how he must have made his approach, and the odds that hovered against him. What he did is beyond imagination and comprehension. I made landfalls at San Salvador, Acklin, Great Isaacs, Puerto Rico, the chain of islands from the American and British Virgins down the Windward-Leeward, the Antilles, to Grenada and Trinidad, the Gulf of Paria, Venezuela, Pargo Bay, Colombia and on and on. To think of his seamanship, if nothing else, but suffering from arthritis and malaria, he pressed on; a driving force was within, pushing him to discovery and to destruction.

I am glad he died without knowing America was named after Amerigo Vespucci—a sad mistake. That would have been too much for him to bear. It is true, however, that all too late, appreciation is shown.

I believe the only reason Columbus did not sail to El Salvador was because it is the only one of the Central American Republics not having a coast on the Caribbean Sea. El Salvador didn't exist under this name until around 1524, one of the few bodies of land he did not name. Its only coast is on the Pacific Ocean. Columbus would have had a difficult land passage to get there. By then, he had much to deter him.

As the anchor came up the next morning before dawn, I bid silent farewell to the last stop north of Columbus' Caribbean adventures. Our next destination, 200 miles up the coast, was to be Honduras. Like many of the countries visited in this chain up from South America, earthquakes have taken a toll. In May of 1951, an earthquake destroyed four of the little country's towns and laid waste to 400 square miles of its area.

The wind swung around from offshore to northwest by west 3/4 west giving us a fair wind, close hauled, for the Gulf of Honduras. Beating up the coast to a warm wind was to *Tamarit*'s liking and ours. She danced to cross-seas, leftovers from a Papagayo and the new seas building to the new northwesterly slant. This action made her surf one long moment then slog into a head sea. After ten miles of this, the seas settled into the steady push of the Nor'wester. I was on watch in the mid-afternoon. Above the masts was a buttermilk cloud pattern interspersed with powder blue sky. A bright sun was aloft lighting the coagulate of clouds and sending unbelievably brilliant shafts of light to the ocean below—like giant backstays. White-capped seas were dancing to the winds that fathered them, pushing and shoving to touch the beautiful schooner that enjoyed their playfulness, when out of a wave shot the entire shimmering blue body of a graceful sailfish glistening with its sail fully extended—its eyes round and sparkling. Only its tail-fin touched the water, gyrating and quivering at great speed, propelling and dancing one of nature's marvels across the crests, its sword within inches of *Tamarit*'s charging bowsprit. It traveled perhaps 80 feet across the bow before its air-dance was completed. A one-act play with a perfect backdrop, the curtain was slow to go down! Applause! Applause! No curtain call but another great moment to remember.

Looking ahead, as darkness fell on a moonless night, I wasn't sure of what I was seeing. In the black distance, the darkness was interrupted by pulsating firelight. Then I knew, for the radio had mentioned earlier that the volcano of Izalco, El Salvador was active. The illumination of its frequent eruptions was visible for a great distance at sea. The commentator had said, "For that reason it was called The Lighthouse of the Pacific or The Lighthouse of Central America." All night we held our course on nature's own lighthouse, sailing toward this dramatic country with 150 rivers and streams that flow into the Pacific and its many volcanoes that add intrigue to the native's life. It was another unforgettable experience. In this part of the world, the "unforgettables" came often and stayed late. I am so fortunate, for I have only to close my eyes and see those grand sights over and over. There is no boredom for me—I have memories; no monotony, for I am inquisitive.

A beautiful world grasped the early light of the rising sun, using it to brighten, polish, burnish and gild this sailor's world. I think the coming of the dawn is something the sailor sees so much more than the landsman. If the most confirmed landsman could be here, I believe he would stir with the sight of this great sweep of green watery world, of wind-lashed rollers crested with foam of cirrus clouds streaked across the heavens and of this tall schooner rolling the sea to leeward. There are few things in life grander than nature, yet people often seem embarrassed to express their reveries. We were closing on the land after a long tack in from the sea and as I stood on the deck, I watched the waves breaking with thunderous crashes and echoing roars on a bold, precipitous bluff, and saw swells rise powerfully to dash to a flustered, frenzied ruin upon the rocks. Graceful birds banked in the early light, scolded and dove for their breakfast. The night had turned to gold, a marvelous transfiguration as the sun came on watch ready for its day's passage to glorify and illuminate our side of the world.

The Gulf of Fonseca lay dead ahead, for land now was on both sides of the bow. Our destination was a cove just inside the bay and inside Amalpa Point, Honduras. It was most interesting to be entering this little gulf. Within our immediate view was Nicaragua. It was one mile from us on our starboard beam as we sailed in. On our starboard bow was Honduras and close by ten beautiful islands just inside the Gulf. Dead ahead was our destination in the Conejos River mouth inside Amalpa Point. We were discovering El Salvador, her backdrop the smoking volcanic cone of Izalco, impressive by day and by night. Reefs, rocks and islands popping up kept us busy navigating by the detail chart, binoculars and a man aloft. As the water flattened in the lee of the land, we dropped the anchor to get a firm hold on Honduras.

The crew furled sails, sluiced down the decks and put her shipshape. Soon bacon, eggs and hot cakes sent their odors up from the galley. *Tamarit* rested surrounded by the volcanic cones of still another volatile world.

It was hot here out of the wind, in the lee of the land, for by now, after two months at sea, we were wind people. After some sleep and a pleasant breakfast, we decided to sail up the coast to La Herradura for the night. This was a good decision, for the wind was pleasant there and under the deck awning we kept cool and rested.

On shore was a quaint, thatched-hut, Spanish-speaking settlement close to the beach. The friendly people greeted us—but were frightened, for they had a rather violent earthquake in the night. They asked if we felt it on the yacht. We hadn't due to the sea action, however, I have felt them on a calm sea and on two occasions, I have been on my boat, very much involved in tidal waves. That was catastrophic.

Earthquakes have ruined their city of San Salvador many times. After each disaster, the people set to work to clear away the debris and rebuild their homes of wood or adobe. Their towns, cities and villages are very attractive with brightly painted homes beneath tile roofs.

We enjoyed this land of mountains, hills, upland plains, rivers, lakes and friendly people. They paddled out to the yacht to give and not to beg. We exchanged things from our different worlds. I pray none of those people will die in the blistering desert of America as happened to those wanting to live in our United States.

Tamarit moved off the anchor under main, foresail, staysail and jib. We were waving to the friendly village people lining the beach showing sad enthusiasm for our departure. Everywhere around the world I have made these departures leaving people of every race and culture standing on their shores waving just like this. My hope is that I will be able to go back to all of them, to take up and renew my friendships. It would take a lifetime but what a great new life it would be. Often, I wonder what my friends are doing in far off Zamboanga, Malekula, Lae, Rabaul, Aruba,

Cartagena, Bora Bora, Tonga, Canton Island, Epi, Bali, Hokaido, Kotsebu, Old Providence, Rotuma, San Blas and on and on. It would be so great to sail back, drop anchor and shake hands once again. I have gone back to some of those places, so I know the pleasantries of the return.

We sailed out offshore fifteen miles on a warm fifteen-knot wind, came about on port tack and beat up the coast bound for Guatemala. Most of our sleeping was on deck with only cotton sheets at the most. Rainsqualls were great. We would throw our pads and sheets below, grab the soap and have a fresh water shower. The squalls lasted longer down in these lower latitudes so we could usually get the soap off. Out in the Pacific on the Transpacific Yacht Races to Hawaii, the rainsqualls were usually short-lived. We would get hair and body lathered up and the rain would stop. Fresh water on the boat being rationed left none for washing, so we wore our soap until the next rainsquall. Once that was a soapy five days.

There are places in the world where rain comes down hard and continues as though never to stop. I have had hard rain experiences in the Philippines and in Panama but nothing like the morning when on my own cutter, under sail, I departed Golfito, Costa Rica, sailed only two miles out when it started to pour—not drops, but solid sheets. It was a new experience. The rain killed the wind it was falling so heavy and for twelve hours the rain didn't stop, nor even waiver. The mainsail caught so much water that a waterfall came off the sail and poured over the boom in absolute torrents. Visibility was zero and stayed zero. The gunnels had wide slit scuppers, well calculated to take care of the volume of water that normally would be evacuated from the surfaces of deck and cabin top, but the rain came so hard and so fast that the water rose above the gunnels. In spite of the scuppers, it poured in almost full boat length sheets over the caprails on both sides. The water held its level of seven inches deep over the decks, for it was constantly replenished for twelve hours. The boat had to be kept battened down and with soggy humidity and no fresh air it was a difficult time below decks. The boat was so clean topside that I opened the water fill aperture on the deck to our drinking water tank and soon ran it over straight from the decks. It was nine o'clock at night before the rain stopped. The wind came to find us and help us continue to sail.

Back on *Tamarit*—after baths, another day and night of sailing brought us to the city of Champerico in Guatemala. This country is most northerly of the five Central American Republics. Its interior is crossed by elevated mountain ranges, with many volcanoes, some of which, like the other countries we have visited, were active. It has short, swift streams and dense tropical forests. It contains some of the most fertile soil in America.

Guatemala is a fascinating country. Mountains occupy two-thirds of its area, the cordillera of the Andes. The highest peak visible from out at sea was Mount Tajumulco, a volcanic peak that rises 13,824 feet. Even Guatemala's valleys scattered among all her peaks have elevations ranging from 5,000 to 8,000 feet. Because of its mountainous character, we found Guatemala presents a great diversity of climate—from an average of 80°F in the lowlands with dense tropical growth to tierra fria in the high altitude, with temperatures that go below the freezing point. This great land, small in area, has a background made interesting by its many ruins and relics of Aztec and Mayan origin, and some even older. Antiqua, Guatemala, the capital founded in 1542, was destroyed by an earthquake. Its citizens migrated to the valley of Ermita and founded the new capital, Guatemala City. It is now digging out from a recent quake. Guatemala's National Observatory has registered as many as 250 earthquakes in a single week. All of the Central American countries have had their political revolutions, pirates, earthquakes and destitution, but I marvel how these people continue to come back and to rise, each time a littler higher. I feel that the "strong family" is the cohesion that makes for Guatemala's friendliness and their drive to succeed. They are very tired of empty promises and Communism—they want stability. With their spirit and their attitude toward God, they will rise. It is hard for them to be patient. The government and the people must rise together—unified.

As Pope John Paul II, on his visit, said to the decision makers, "Apply your power, whether it is political, economic or cultural, in the service of the solidarity of all mankind, especially the most needy whose rights are most often violated. Place yourselves on the side of the poor—give them land. God intended that the people have land. When the poor have land, they can rise. Dignity is so important."

This was our day to leave Guatemala and enter the extreme lower latitude of the waters controlled by Mexico. Mexico also counts hundreds of volcanic cones. In a cornfield there is a cone 1,345 feet high that sprouted in 1943.

Of greater and graver importance to us, however, was the immediate area we were entering—the dreaded Gulf of Tehuantepec and those vicious winds, 'The Tehuantepeckers'. The Sailing Directions are precise, and rightfully so: "Do not cut across the Gulf. Follow the coastline a quarter of a mile off the beach. Hug the land all the way around." This I was prepared to do as we departed Champerico, which is the beginning of the cut as the land falls away to form the Gulf.

There was about eight miles an hour of wind, so we were with the mainsail, foresail, staysail, jib, and the engine—motor sailing. *Tamarit* was well inshore, hugging the beach in the lee of the cliffs. The high velocity hot winds are to be avoided as they come screaming off the Bank of Campeche, the Gulf of Mexico and the Caribbean. These vicious winds venture across the narrow isthmus and shoot out into the Pacific Ocean. The gale force winds blow over the vessels as they hug the cliffs and the beach the full length of the huge Gulf.

It was hot and Mr. Tenny was anxious. There was little or no wind so he said, "This is a waste of time. Let's cut across."

"It is a mistake," I said, "I know this place, please read what the Sailing Directions indicate."

"Let's cut across, I'll be responsible," he insisted.

"It is your boat, but it is a mistake."

Mr. Tenny took the helm and sailed out on his new course to take us off shore to the middle of the Gulf to save time and distance traveled. We hadn't covered but two and a half miles when all Hell broke loose. The gale force hot blasts came down on us and turned the sea mottled and streaked with foaming torn white caps. In one big push, *Tamarit* couldn't get her speed up. Before she could move out— WHAM! The bronze turnbuckle securing the head stay at the bow broke in two. The stay, the boom and the staysail went shooting into the sky then down they came flailing the mast, the shrouds, the lifelines and stanchions. It was vicious—and to be on the foredeck was deadly. That wildly swinging boom nearly got me. The staysail exploded into ribbons and went skyward again. While that scene was going on, the good mainsail tore from leach to tack through the center of the sail. It was in two large pieces for a short half minute, then it became many more. The violent snapping and luffing of the upper half of the sail flipped the halyard off the sheave at the top of the mainmast, so we couldn't lower the upper part of the sail. The mainsail flapped and snapped to ribbons and threads. The lower half attached to the violently swinging main boom was busy tearing itself to bits and shreds, beating against the main shrouds and stanchions.

Suffice it to say, it was embarrassing! No one spoke. Bob and I had our work cut out getting that wild, chaotic picture framed and hung. Riding aloft in the bos'n's chair, freeing the flapping, tearing mainsail and the fouled halyard was wild and exhausting. Several hours of work alow and aloft were spent getting the sails down, bending on new sails and jurying up the head stay. The staysail boom and the foremast were badly dented and skinned. It was all in a minutes work for a Tehuantepecker. Mexico came on like a lion for Henry the Lamb.

We stayed at sea for the next 310 miles, back to the routine of watches day and night. Our next port of call would be Acapulco. Sailing was steady slogging into the seas for the next three days. Fishing was very good, and I found that trolling at 6.5 knots under sail is ideal. One year, I recall, we took the largest albacore for the season while trolling under sail using a feather jig. Another cruise, off Ceralvo Island in the Sea of Cortez, I landed a Wahoo just six feet in length on a hand trolling line with a feather jig. A Wahoo hits hard, fights hard and makes it difficult for whomever is on the other end of the hand line, especially if he is without gloves. The Wahoo looks very much like a Barracuda, having long, sharp teeth but a heavier body. They also frequent the Atlantic where I have caught them in the Gulf Stream. One cruise near the Isla de Coiba, off the West Coast of Panama, I was trolling with my 1,000-yard reel, using 108-pound test line. We were under sail, moving at three knots, when the reel began singing as line went running out. I sat on the deck, threw on my harness, snapped it to the reel and went to work. I clamped down on the drag and settled in for a workout. My wife dropped the sails; the boat was a 38 foot cutter of heavy displacement. To my astonishment, the boat stopped with a heavy pull aft and started making stern way, a 15 ton boat. Whatever it was on the line, we didn't have need nor room for it on board. It was too big to gaff and when I finally got it close enough to see it eye-to-eye-a Tiger Shark—I knew I didn't want it. (I have caught and landed a 600-pound shark so no, thanks!) This one was as tired as I was but looked madder. I estimated he would weigh at least 900 pounds and I didn't want him to lash out or charge the planks of the boat. My wife got the knife from the scabbard hanging just inside the hatchway and cut the line. All three of us were relieved. That line, rod, and reel, by the way, caught and landed a 1,036-1/2 pound white death shark off the Great Barrier Reef of Australia.

Acapulco, Mexico, was dead ahead at 0900. We got shipshape. The Mexican flag was at the starboard spreader. The yellow quarantine flag was flying below it, and on the staff aft we carried the American flag. We entered Boca Grande and sailed on into the Bahia de Acapulco. We hadn't seen this much activity, this many people, and this many cantilevered structures for months. It was a little overwhelming. Speedboats screamed around us. Paddleboards, bikinis, yachts, Customs and Immigration officers on boats crowded our approach. All cleared, we went around the Punta Grifo and tied up at the Club de Yates guest dock. An entirely different attitude was noticed. We had met the people of the Central Americas and all wanted to give and share. Here it was such a contrast—everyone wanted money.

While lying at the busy dock the next day with yachts and many people, the very loud loudspeaker came on. The voice said, "Captain Adams, come to the office—bring money!!"

We now had 1,431 nautical miles to go, all up hill against the prevailing wind. We took on water, provisions and got our customs clearance, but the Mexicans could not supply us with diesel fuel, which was important to Henry to meet his new schedule. He had called home and his attorney advised his early arrival in California. Our only chance for diesel fuel would be at Manzanillo, the next port to the north. Henry phoned ahead to the Port Captain at Manzanillo to see if there would be fuel. Yes, there was, but that was a mistake, as we were to learn later.

I have found in Mexico, 'Don't eat it unless you can peel it,' has stood me in good stead to avoid amoebic dysentery.

Mexico has made big strides in clearing up this problem, however, in some areas the problem remains. Amoebic dysentery is common in the tropics and has been quite common in Mexico until recent years. I believe that infection is acquired by ingestion of food or drink contaminated by feces that contain the amoebic cysts. Food handlers often are carriers, who at times may not have diarrhea. This can be a principal source. Transmission can involve direct contact with contaminated food, or unwashed hands. Flies and cockroaches can be carriers from contact with faulty plumbing. In suspect areas, one should use caution in bathing, and washing teeth, fish, vegetables, or fruit with polluted water. In my travels around the world I have never been without Halizone, or equivalent, water treatment tablets. On boats, a few pellets dropped in the fresh water tanks are good insurance. Even in off-the-beaten-path restaurants, or when drinking from wells or rivers, a few pellets in the drinking container can save hours, days, or even months of real and genuine discomfort, possibly total debility. On a boat, confined, and under stresses of responsibility to function physically and mentally, this infectious disease should be avoided at all costs. The pleasures derived from taking the chance that it won't happen are not worth the anguish and suffering. I have been there, I know, for I lost 30 pounds and had the problem for four months while sailing to the West Indies from California after a stop in Ylapa, Mexico.

While in Acapulco, we noticed a boat loaded with prisoners departing for the prison at Tres Maris Islands. The sails on the vessel were in poor condition. Henry inquired where the prison authorities were located and found them. He presented them with our blown out mainsail and staysail, and gave them two other sails for which he would have no further use. The Mexicans were most appreciative for they operated the prison boat on a very tight, locked-up budget. With barely enough diesel fuel and our head stay fixed, we departed after four days of perusing Mexico's Acapulco, the Queen Resort for the jet set. Acapulco has something for everyone—a broad range. It was interesting to see the ships from the Orient bringing in and departing with all types of products. People from Canada, Bolivia, England, the Estados Unidos and others have helped with their dollars and Mexico's foresight to make the Mexican coast one of this half of the earth's finest resort and vacationlands. Millionaires and billionaires are creating marble floored villas for those who can afford it—those who want luxury and privacy.

I had previously sailed down to Las Cruces, inside the tip of the Baja Peninsula, and spent ten days with Bing Crosby at his Las Cruces estate on the Sea of Cortez. It was a pleasure to have fished with Mr. Crosby on his yacht *Dorado*, catch marlin and, in turn, to take him for his first sailboat ride out to Ceralvo Island. We later flew in his DC-3 around the Peninsula from Las Cruces to La Paz and to Palmilla. His remark, as we watched the sea and terrain below, was, "This will be the playground of the United States one day. Mexico's Pacific Coast is alive with the future—resorts, guitars, fish, rivieras, and oil. Mexico is rising. Ensenada will become another San Diego—and will control the tuna industry."

The wind was zero as we proceeded up the coast under power and sail. It was hot and our diesel fuel was getting progressively more rare in the tanks. As we departed Acapulco, I looked over to starboard to see the fine, old yacht *Corsair*, formerly owned by the wealthy Mr. Pierpont Morgan. Reportedly, a drunken Mexican crew had run her on the rocks. Her handsome bow was sticking out of the breaking seas; a sad demise for what was, in her day, one of the finest luxury yachts of the United States.

By 0900 the next morning, *Tamarit* had Punta Las Ventanas abeam and we started making our turn to enter Manzanillo Bay. There, under the point of land, was a pilot vessel that moved out quickly to meet us. They waved, came alongside and put a pilot on board, and proceeded ahead of us toward the Manzanillo breakwater. We ran up our quarantine flag under the Mexican flag, lowered our sails and got shipshape, not realizing the extent of this welcoming. We got our fenders out, secured our dock lines and proceeded to the fuel dock as indicated by the pilot. Two Mexicans were standing on the dock with friendly smiles. With arm signals made with their arms extended, they indicated for my crew to toss the bow and stern lines to them. They received our lines and secured them to the cleats on the dock. I said, "Gracias, amigos."

Another Mexican came from the fuel dock office and handed down the diesel fuel hose. We took on 250 gallons of diesel No. 2. That finished, Mr. Tenny proceeded up to the office to pay the bill. Then came the big surprise. In his telephone conversation from Acapulco all he had asked was, "Do you have diesel No. 2? We will arrive tomorrow morning."

"Tamarit"—photo by Al Adams, Skipper—1946

He was handed a bill for $1500.00 all itemized. The pilot boat—so many dollars, plus overtime. The pilot boat crew—four men, plus overtime—waiting for our arrival. The two line handlers on the dock we thought were just being courteous—wages for their service was on the bill. The man who handed down the hose and later hauled it back up—wages for that service was added to the bill. Then the charge for the diesel fuel was indicated. Services and fuel—$1500.00. (Note: the fuel wouldn't have been more than $100.00.)

The fuel was in the tank. We had no recourse. Mexico—*bring money*!! Mr. Tenny was fuming. He was going to write his Congressman. He was going to, going to . . . ! I never heard how he came out. It is too bad a few greedy people spoil the association with the great Mexican people who are not that way. We departed Manzanillo with a bad taste. It is a beautiful resort.

Tamarit had faired us well. It is difficult to beat the time that we had made covering 5,000 miles in 2½ months. We had been to many places, many different countries and enjoyed so many associations with the people it would be difficult to meet traveling in any other way. The rest of the Mexican coast was covered with no stops to meet Mr. Tenny's appointment in Los Angeles. *Tamarit* sailed into San Diego Harbor and we were cleared at the Customs and Immigration stations. We proceeded to the San Diego Yacht Club where *Tamarit* took up residency. She was a great schooner and a great addition to the Club's fleet. She had made reality of my dream stuff.

"Tamarit"—photo by Al Adams, Skipper—1946

*It is a pleasant force one feels that would
have him sail away over the horizon
and follow the sun and a star
to the ends of the earth.*

Tamarit anchored at Todos Santos Island.
Photo by Jim Delorey—1964

Tamarit
Photo by Al Adams, Skipper—1946

Note: The cruise of the TAMARIT to the West Coast was covered in a motion picture taken by the author. This film was shown on the Jack Douglas television program "Golden Voyage."

Tamarit
Photos by Al Adams, Skipper—1946

Tamarit under sail in San Francisco Bay.
Photo from the collection of Jim Delorey—1961

When It All Happens

A Story
Depicting the Trials and Tribulations
Of a Charter Boat Skipper

Stella Maris II

Stella Maris II
Photo from Al Adams collection. Original taken by W.C. Sawyer.
Courtesy of Newport Harbor Nautical Museum.

WHEN IT ALL HAPPENS

These people were from Bakersfield, California, which perhaps contributed to the events destined to occur at sea on this cruise. Living that distance of inland miles is a factor in people's thinking as well as their actions and reactions. Taking people out of their surroundings and way of daily living, plus depositing them on *Stella Maris II*, a 54' ketch, can be too much or maybe not enough. There are a lot of unknowns.

These were fine people, down-to-earth and intelligent, who had heard of my sailing instruction operation of taking parties to and through the Channel Islands off the Southern California coast. This sounded interesting to them. Their letter indicated 24 in their group, fellows and their ladies, for three days of sailing over the Fourth of July weekend, time of arrival in San Pedro 0800. With their letter was a holding check and a note, "Tell us what to bring." They wanted to bring all the food and beverages indicating they were readily adaptable to any condition, being an active, fun-loving group. I wrote giving them the boat's layout, number of bunks, deck space, location of the boat marina, the slip number and suggested proper sailing clothing.

My crew was Hilda. She and I arrived early that Saturday, washed down the boat, fueled up, checked the stove, iced the ice chest, removed the sail covers and warmed up the diesel engine. The head was working, the bilge was okay and all was in readiness. The party arrived with boxes of food, sleeping bags, fishing poles, golf clubs, a steamer trunk and a French poodle. One girl had a hatbox, another was carrying a hair dryer, her hair was in curlers and she was wearing bedroom slippers.

Well, Hilda and I gulped and went about helping to organize the stowing. All were friendly and anxious to help. The girls got together with Hilda while I did what I could to orient the fellows. A first, and a very important must, was to immediately invite the girls to the head, and in explicit detail, explain the function of the sea-going toilet facility. I stressed nothing, absolutely nothing, was to go into the toilet unless it had previously been eaten. This was a most unusual way to begin introductions and friendships with twelve girls (and a poodle). By now all were looking over my shoulder. I was down on my knees, my chin nearly resting on the bowl explaining one must open this valve first which, in conjunction with the pump handle being worked rather vociferously, would allow the contents of the bowl to begin evacuation. But, before pumping, open this other smaller valve, which will allow flushing water into the bowl as the pump is being gyrated. Then, girls, when the by-products of metabolism have disappeared, turn off the little valve. Pump five more times and clear the bowl and pump mechanism, then close the big valve. Did all of you follow that? If not, let's go through it again. Now, the don'ts. Do not use an excessive amount of toilet paper, which will clog the pump and the lines. Do not put bobby pins, hairpins or sanitary napkins into the bowl. Remember, girls, only if it has been partaken orally does it go in the bowl. One mistake and this whole diabolic mechanism and the sea valve have to be taken apart. It is awful, not unlike playing squat tag in a cesspool and there are no plumbers at sea. After that lesson, I rose up and formally met each girl.

I went through the same procedure with the fellows.

We then went topside to acquaint the group with the standing and running rigging. They had indicated they would be the crew. Since there is at least 'one in every crowd,' I had only to look and he was there. His name was

Herman and he wore a white yachting cap with bright brass buttons and an airplane insignia on the front. The other was his girl friend, Militia, the one with the poodle. She, Herman, and the yipping poodle! But I must be patient.

It was becoming more obvious that I must keep an eye on Herman who announced he had once sailed on a boat four years ago. He was now in the process of showing everyone all he didn't know. It was showing up in his conversation and his un-nautical vocabulary such as, "Avast the square sail! Splice the gunnels! Box the binnacle!" and this next one I hadn't heard before as he related a sea story out of his one-time sailing past. "I was the only one on the foredeck. It was a helluva blow but it had to be done. I spliced the brace." Further, he explained to his poodle-bearing, wide-eyed girlfriend, "Those belaying pins on that boat over there are for fighting off pirates and the left side of the boat is the larboard and the right is the garboard." Incredible. I, too, was learning.

Other eyebrows in the group were raised along with mine but no one argued these sage points. Maybe he would just run down.

He needed something to do. I asked him if he would bend the jib. He told me he had never bent one but he would snap it on the shrouds. I told him it would be better if he hanked it on the jib stay instead and handed him the bagged jib.

A final check below was made to see if all their gear was stowed in good order, and checked the head, the bilge, the crankcase oil, and water cooling reservoir on the diesel, and as I came up out of the hatch, I noticed the rigging was shaking violently. Looking forward, there was the answer. Herman had scandalized the jib! It was hanked on the wrong stay upside down and riding high in the wind. The sheets were whipping my neighbor's boat. The owner was cussing, for he was varnishing his rail and, brush in hand, was dodging the snapping lines.

We got the jib down, rebent it on the jib stay and secured it with gaskets. I then rove the jib sheets through the fairleads. I went aft to start the engine and asked two of the fellows to stand by to cast off the port bow and stern lines. The wind was coming in over the starboard quarter aft. Helpful Herman was on the bowsprit. I bent over to stow a line in the lazarette when a loud splash occurred forward. I peered over the rail to see a white yachting cap floating at the scene of the swash. The girlfriend was hysterical and the dog was barking wildly. The inwardly chuckling crew dragged aboard Bubbling Herman. The excited, barking dog bit him. The first aid kit was brought out but the patient was only nipped—no blood, no teeth marks. He insisted on a bandage. His girlfriend gave him mouth-to-mouth resuscitation and changed his clothes.

Finally! All was in readiness. I turned the key, tried the starter and—it was stuck. The guests registered those ghastly question marks, while I unconcernedly burned. Up came the floor boards, then for 30 minutes I stood on my head in the bilge taking apart the starter to free the Bendix. The guests were poking their heads down the hatches, plugging the companionway, and offering advice and all-too-numerous ideas on what was wrong. The pessimistic gal with the dog just knew it was too good to be true that they were going to Catalina Island on a boat.

The starter was fixed but my clothes were in bad shape. I had grease to my elbows, and was god-awful hot and perspiring. While cleaning up I glanced out the porthole. Two of my party were out in the dinghy looking in the portholes of my other neighbor's yacht. The owner, in his pajamas, had poked his head out of the hatch to register marked abhorrence!

At last out of the anchorage we went as Hilda and I made sail. One of the fellows took the helm. The sails filled away to a freshening southwest wind. The engine was stopped. We rounded the lighthouse and held a course for Avalon, Santa Catalina Island. Shirts were coming off. One of the fellows named Marco was a Mr. Muscles. He was flexing and posing, and his girl was so proud. The group was settled on the decks and cabin top 'enjoying' and smearing suntan lotion on each other. They were excited with the spray and the angle of heel. It was beautiful sailing weather with no clouds in an unusually blue sky. A large ship was off to port inside the crisp western horizon and coming with a bone in her teeth. A school of anchovies kept a flock of sea gulls, cormorants and pelicans busy diving and scolding.

The party was getting the feel of the motion of the ketch. Two others went to the rail. Herman was subdued and resting his head in his girlfriend's lap which he shared with the poodle.

A few miles out to sea and a call for help came from below. I asked Herman to steer 110° until I could return. Well, here was one of the ladies in the head busier than a cat on a tin roof. I could hear her opening and closing valves, pumping and panting and in her anguish was muttering, "Don't come up any higher." It was a standard rule with me that when water starts running out from under the head door onto the carpeted main salon, I intervene.

Now mutual embarrassment existed as I hadn't known her long enough to attach a name. I pumped and explained the procedure once again and then mopped the floor.

Hurrying back on deck, I found Hilda trying to tell Herman we were heading back toward land, that we were hove to in the path of that oncoming steamer.

"Thanks, Herman, I'll take the helm," and I jibed her as the steamer's loud horn sounded three blasts to indicate her engine's were full astern.

We moved out of the steamer's path as the deck officer called down through his megaphone, "It would be better if you didn't fish in the fairway."

Embarrassing.

To this point we had met all challenges. We were making over eight knots and the wind was great. In the middle of the Catalina channel, Herman's girl wanted to go swimming, so then everyone wanted to go swimming. I dropped the sails and put out the swim boarding ladder.

Twenty-four bodies donned swimsuits and the splash fest began. This takes a lot of vigilance on the part of a skipper, for the "pool" was deeper and larger out there than Bakersfield people realized. The swim party went well until Kent, one of the fellows, decided to dive off the bowsprit. He climbed up the bobstay to the foredeck, up the hard way hanging on the whisker shrouds. He lifted his body over the cap rail, stood up and his wet foot stepped on the varnished king plank, center of the foredeck—wham! His right forearm went under the fluke of the bow anchor, which was secured in chocks on the deck. Wincing with pain, he sat up with his hand bent back in a very unnatural attitude. It was obvious his wrist or forearm was broken. Everyone gathered around as the swim party was over.

"Kent," I said, "we are halfway to the island and it is your decision. I will either take you back to the mainland to a doctor, or on to Avalon where, hopefully, we can locate a doctor on this busy vacation weekend."

His decision, "Let's go to Avalon."

Up went the sails and on went the engine. We would motor sail to get aid. Hilda was at the helm. She was great help on the boat and a fine helmsperson. As we sailed, I studied Kent. He was hurting but saying nothing. He should have the break set and a cast installed. This was something I hadn't done before. On one of these charter trips I had delivered a baby. I had administered to a fellow having an epileptic seizure. I had helped rescue and revive a scuba diver who was down too long, but I had never set a broken arm.

"Kent," I said, "I have never administered to this condition but I will if you wish." He was relieved with the idea that someone would help.

"Great, would you give it a try? I can't move my fingers and the arm is cramped."

Three fellows of the crew were called, one to wrap his arms around Kent's chest holding him against the roll of the boat, another to hold his bicep very firmly with two hands, and the other to hold Kent's forearm steady with both hands. Grasping Kent's hand, much as I would in shaking one's hand, I braced against his bicep with my left hand, alerted all concerned and pulled the hand out at the angle it was bent. It responded with a pop which was encouraging to all as with it he could move his fingers.

"Let's do that again."

All assembled and took their places as I pulled the hand again in line with the new attitude and it popped. Kent felt relieved. From the First Aid Kit I acquired an ace bandage and a sling, and bound his arm and hand using a cardboard splint.

Swelling had started so the tension of the ace was relieved at intervals as we sailed.

We arrived at Avalon in the afternoon and were assigned a mooring. The patient felt okay so he didn't bother to find a doctor. We had a fine dinner, which the girls prepared. As evening came on, everyone appeared on deck in his or her party clothes and by shore boat service, we were off to the Casino for dancing.

Approaching Casino at Avalon
Photo from Al A.Adams collection

It was decided which part of the veranda we would call home base so we could look down over the romantic bay to the ketch in the rising moon's path.

Kent danced and it was prearranged that we would meet every other dance to adjust his arm bandage to allow for the swelling. Better if he would rest the arm as I was concerned about numbness but he said he had good feeling in all sections of his hand when I lightly stuck him with a pin. Setting a bone without X-rays of the break could be very serious. A sharp bone break could sever a nerve; especially in the setting procedure such as we had done under the rolling boat movement at eight plus knots. As I had mentally reviewed the symptoms at the time of the break, there was reason to suspect a broken bone because Kent couldn't move the injured part. The arm had been bent in an odd attitude and there was pain when he tried to move his arm and fingers. There was lack of feeling when touched plus swelling and blueness of the skin. The problem in review was how many hours would go by before medical attention; thus, a decision was made to do the bone setting procedure.

It was a beautiful moonlit scene there on the Casino veranda overlooking the sparkling sea as the orchestra completed its romantic titillations. A pleasant excitement remained as the music diminished into the night.

Only *compleat* lovers, in tune with such pleasures, would know these precious feelings, these great moments of endearment that mortals try to grasp unto themselves, not wanting the plateau, so seldom reached, to slip away.

A rare night it was. The group started arriving back at the yacht by shore boat in twos and fours. By 2 a.m., all had bedded down in bunks, on deck or in the passageways. Herman and Militia were the last to arrive and Herman was more than pleasantly inebriated. His wide-eyed blond was also without pain. I helped her flow off the shore boat. The night was yet young for them. The plateau was still in their grasp as they clung to each other, embracing and stroking.

Trying to be subtle, I found their sleeping bags and suggested they sleep on the cockpit cushions. With that I returned to my cabin, closed the door and turned in.

They were noisily moving about, awakening everyone, but I said, "Patience, Adams," and dozed off.

A loud knock on my cabin door came just as I had greeted Morpheus, the God of Dreams. It was Herman. I lit my cabin light to reveal his countenance much besmeared with lipstick.

"Skipper," he said, "will you marry us?"

"No, Herman. You can get the Justice of the Peace in the morning."

"Please, Skipper, we must get married now! *Hic!* We are at sea and the captain of the ship can marry people."

"But, Herman," I replied, groping for a way out, "we are not beyond the twelve mile limit."

"Yes we are, *hic!* It is 20 miles over here, so can we get started?"

This was not going to be concluded without a ceremony of some kind so I climbed out and dressed. Herman was now uncontrollably happy, rousing everyone. The lights went on, the dog barked and a pajama party gathered in the main salon. Twenty-six people and a dog crowded onto the bunks and settees. It was most festive, and to add to the occasion, out came a large can of Jolly Time popcorn and a bottle of champagne.

Well, I was on the spot. The only way to get some sleep was to get it done. So, I put my blue wool sailing shirt on backwards. There was no Bible on board, so I chose the book in the navigator's library titled "United States Coast Pilot-North Pacific."

As the popcorn can went around among the pajama-clad bodies, I stood with my back to the mainmast where it came through the cabin top down through the cabin sole. Herman and his quivering Militia knelt on the carpet before me. It was a serious joke. Too serious.

Suddenly there was quiet. I gulped; the world was waiting for me to begin something that shouldn't be. It was an awful moment, one that few people have the pleasure of experiencing.

How should I start? What is said on these occasions? Then I heard myself speak: "We are gathered here to join this couple in Holy Matrimony. They have made known their desire to enter into wedlock. Is there a best man who will step forward and is there a maid of honor?"

From the group came a pajama-clad couple and they took their places to complete the bridal group. I continued, "Is there anyone who will come forward who has cause to terminate this marriage?"

No one spoke. Now, I hoped to find a loophole to aid me in stopping this union.

"Herman, will you place the bride's ring on the book?"

Sure enough, he dug around and came up with the ring. I gulped.

"Herman, do you take Militia to be your wedded wife?"

A loud "Yes!" from Herman.

"Militia, do you take Herman to be your wedded husband?"

Militia swooned as she looked into Herman's eyes and said, "Yesss."

"This ring, Herman, place it on Militia's finger."

He placed the ring on her finger.

"I pronounce you man and wife. Herman you may kiss the bride."

It was a devastating clinch. The party came alive with congratulations, bride-kissing and poodle-barking.

I retired to my cabin anxious to get a couple of hours sleep. The party settled down. I lulled off to sleep. A timid little knock on my cabin door brought me awake to say, "What now?"

It was Herman and Militia. Herman spoke, "Skipper, *hic*, could we have your cabin?"

Then I did gulp, 'Jeez,' I thought, 'What have I done? They have taken this for real.' I wanted to say NO!

Militia said, "Please, Skipper," her innocent wide eyes pleading.

I took my sleeping bag and walked topside, found a spot on deck between bodies and tried to put matrimony out of my mind. It wasn't easy.

Dawn broke all too quickly. A fine breakfast was begun. Everyone arrived but Herman and Militia. About 1100 hours, as the group was dining, reminiscing and planning their day, the door to my cabin opened and there was lipstick-smeared Herman and his "bride" wedged tightly in one sleeping bag looking out at the breakfasting congregation. They were deliriously happy!

The following morning was spent readying the yacht for the return sail to San Pedro. All in all, the remainder of our stay had gone fairly well. I had been a sea-going plumber only three times which I thought was a good conservative average.

We cast off the mooring lines at 1200 hours and made sail to a 20-knot wind. It was one of those perfect sails on a beam reach. We maintained hull speed of 9 plus knots with no seasickness; an exhilarating sail. Kent's arm was in a sling. He was doing quite well. The poodle was nestled down with the newlyweds in my cabin. A birthday cake was baking in the galley stove for Kent's girl. We would have cake at the dock. It has been an eventful sojourn.

We were about 2 miles out from the San Pedro lighthouse, standing up on a broad reach doing 9 knots. I called for attention from the 24 person crew and suggested that if they wished to save confusion at the dock, it would be well to start pulling their gear, clothes and sleeping bags together. Perhaps half of the group could go below first and the other half later. They were most agreeable. All of them went below to begin packing. The main salon was full of people.

We were sailing fast, reaching, with the yacht standing up due to the wind being on our port side abaft the beam and freshening.

In anticipation of rounding the lighthouse, I called down the hatch and alerted all below that the boat would very shortly round the lighthouse, would go on the wind and heel over with her starboard rail down.

"Don't be concerned, just be alerted."

I trimmed the sails in to go on the wind. The charter guests were laughing, joking, packing, and so crowded in the main salon they were probably dressing each other.

Hilda was at the helm and she called out, "Stand by to come on the wind! Ready! Coming up!" and we rounded the lighthouse. We went rail down.

Well, the crowning touch, the awful truth, there was a lady in the head. The head was on the port side and suddenly became the high side when we heeled to starboard. The lady was sitting in the head unaware of the pending change. She flipped off the seat hit the head door, forced the latch, the door flew open, she hit the step, and bounded on her bare buttocks out onto the carpet with her ankles next to her ears. She stopped in the center of the crowded salon with her string-bikini around one ankle. The final touch: In her hand was a carefully folded pad of tissues—four fingers on one side and her thumb on the other.

Some said it was "Unreal." But, no. It was real.

It was a grand finale to a weekend of "When It All Happens." No strings attached!

Kent called me from Bakersfield the next day to tell me his doctor x-rayed the arm and commented, "Whoever set your arm saved you a lot of money!"

I was much relieved to learn the doctor just put his arm in a cast. And relieved in a much different way when Herman called to say his mother had insisted that he and Militia be married on shore and right away. Whew!

Editor's Acknowledgements

This has been a very interesting project. The greatest enjoyment for me was the fantastic networking between people with some sort of connection. All of these connections played a part in the completion of this book. I will ramble on . . .

I found that there is a special camaraderie between people who have experienced time on a particular boat—not necessarily experiencing that time together, but even at different times on the same boat. I thank Jim Delorey, Dean Spinanger and George Aid for their input regarding *Tamarit*. Their time with her was during the 60's. I thank the current owner, skipper, and crew of *Tamarit* (now named *Shearwater*) Tom Berton, Angus McCamy, and Keith MacKenzie. I also want to thank Maynard Bray of *Woodenboats* for his suggestions regarding research on the *Vayu*.

The friends of Al Adams are definitely a special group. Most of them are fellow Adventurers and have accomplished remarkable lifestyles and adventures of their own. I have enjoyed the communications very much. Thank you, Steve Waterford, Robert Gilliland, Roy Roush, Max Hurlbut, Don Clothier and Bill Muff.

It seems as though it is your own friends and family that get the most abuse sometimes. My own friends were a tremendous help to me. First thanks goes to Jay Rush, my husband, who was always there with suggestions, answers and support. Also I want to thank my singing buddy, Angela Boland, who did the tedious editing from cover to cover. Other friends who helped with proofing, pictures, opinions, etc., were: Tom Mooneyham, Bonnie Keithly, Joyce Reese, Michelle Baker, Margaret Kaplan, Joy Bower, David Miller, Lynn and Keith Chase, and of course, Dianne Adams. We did it!!

Michelle Rush

Glossary of Terms

Abaft	towards the stern
Ahull	sails furled and the helm lashed alee allows the boat to ride to the waves and wind direction.
Alee	away from the direction of the wind
Aloft	up the ship's mast
Alow	low near the deck
Astern	at the back of or behind the ship
Backstay	part of the standing rigging leading aft to support the mast
Ballast	heavy material—usually gravel or lead—placed in the bottom of the boat for greater stability
Bare poles	when the vessel is underway without sails set
Beam ends	a ship on her beam ends is lying so far over she is in danger of capsizing
Beaufort scale	wind force values used to indicate velocity
Bent	to indicate that a sail is secured to its proper place ready for use
Bilge	lowest depths of the ship's hold
Binnacle	a non-magnetic container adjacent to the helm for the compass
Boat	a seaman's term for a small craft

Bobstay	chain or heavy wire rigging from the end of the bowsprit to the stem—mast support
Bone in her teeth	white foam created at the bow by forward motion
Boatswain or Bos'n	a petty officer, usually a good sailor, who inspects ship's sails and rigging
Bo'sun's chair	(boatswain-bo's'n) seat to carry a man aloft in the rigging
Boom	a long spar that extends perpendicular to the mast
Bow	front of the ship
Bowsprit	heavy spar projecting forward from the vessel to aid in setting headsails
Brace	a group
Broach	a dangerous situation—vessel swings to the wind when running free—cause, heavy seas or poor steering
Burgee	flag pennant of a yacht club
Center of effort	the point through which the sum of the driving forces appear to act
Chain plates	strong metal straps set in the sides of a vessel to take the strain of the rigging
Ciquatera Syndrome	poisonous toxin ingested and stored by fish in their flesh
Close-hauled	sails pulled in as tight as possible to allow ship to sail close to the wind
Combers	high rolling and curling sea waves
Dolphin striker	a small spar beneath the bowsprit—a spreader truss to support the bowsprit
Dory	a flat bottomed sea worthy small boat with sharp sheer
Esculent	perhaps questionably edible

Evil spirit	a name given to hurricanes
Fairleads	a block giving a line a fair lead to properly trim a sail the lead reduces or prevents chafe
Fair lead sheet blocks	blocks providing proper angles of the lines or sheets trimming sails
Fall off	steer away from the direction of the wind
Fantail	the space in the overhang of the stern
Fisherman	a light sail whose head hoists to the top of main mast
Flotsam	floating goods
Forecastle or fo'c'sle	raised deck at front of the ship. Also used to describe crewmen—fo'c'sle hand—whose quarters were below this deck
Foremast	the mast farthest forward on a ship
Foresail	on a schooner, that sail set from the foremast. Also seen (and pronounced) as for'sail or fors'l.
Forte	one's strong point
Foundered	to fill with water and sink, to cause to sink
Furl	to roll up and secure a sail on a spar or boom
Gaff	the spar that stands or hoists on the afterside of the mast and supports the head of the sail
Galley	where meals are prepared aboard ship
Gallows	sturdy notched boom support when sail is secured
Gantline	a block and tackle jig secured aloft to raise or lower a man in a boatswain's chair

Garboard	the length of plank next to the keel
Gaskets	bands of canvas by which sails, when furled, are made fast to a boom
Genoa	large jib that usually overlaps the main shrouds
Gollywobbler	a four cornered light air reaching sail hauled to the main masthead of a schooner
Gunwale (gunnel)	the rail of a boat
Halyards	lines for hoisting sails
Handybilly	a simple hand operated pump
Hanks	fittings secured to the luffs of headsails and staysails for bending the sails to the stays
Hatch	opening in a vessel's deck
Hawse hole	the opening in the hause pipe through which the anchor chain or line runs
Hawse pipe	the casting in the bow through which the anchor chain or line runs
Hawser	a heavy line used in kedging, warping or towing
Head	the compartment with toilet facilities
Heel	when the ship leans over in the wind
Helmsman	the sailor who steers the ship
Hog/Hogged	vessel disformed upward amidships from too much stress on rigging pulling planks upward in the area of chain plates
Hove to	to lay the vessel on the wind with the helm to leeward sails trimmed so she comes up and falls off heading up out of the trough for the easy ride

Jib	a triangular sail set forward of the foremast
Jib stay	the stay leading down from aloft on the foremast to which the jib is set
Jibe	when a ship is running before the wind and changes direction, the booms and spars have to be swung from one side of the ship to the other. If badly performed, the ship will broach
Jurying	the expedient in the way of spars and sails in order to bring a vessel to port when disabled
Ketch	a sailing vessel with two masts; the mizzen is forward of the rudder post
King plank	the center notched deck plank into which the other deck planks join
Knot	a measurement of speed over the water, slightly faster than miles per hour. Derived from knots tied in a line at fixed intervals (every forty-seven feet, three inches). Streamed over the side, timed against a twenty-eight-second sand glass, the line measures "knots", or nautical miles per hour.
Larboard	formerly the left side of a vessel, changed to port
Lazarette	a space below decks usually aft used for storage
Leach	the after side of a fore and aft sail
Lee Shore	a shore that is downwind. A ship can be pushed down on a lee shore by a gale

Leeward	the side of a ship that is away from the wind
Leeway	the drift of a ship to leeward of the course being steered
Luff	the forward side of a fore and aft sail
Mainsheet	a line used to control or trim the mainsail
Marconi	lofty triangular sail hoisted to top of main mast
Marine survey	inspection by a qualified person or persons to determine seaworthiness, value and insurability of a vessel
Marlin, Marline	two stranded tarred or creosoted string stuff laid up left-handed for securing, seizing or tying
Mizzen	the after mast of a ketch or yawl from which the mizzen sail is carried—the sail is referred to as the mizzen
Oakum	a caulking material made of tarred or creasoted rope fibers
Oleaginous	oily, greasy, unctuous
Outer Jib	that just beyond the inner jib or jib
Painter	the line in the bow of a boat for towing or making fast
Pawl	a short piece of iron hinged by a pin at one end and secured to the windlass. As the windlass revolves the pawl is dragged along the pawl rim and falls into the pocket indents to prevent any backward motion or running out of chain
Plimsol Marks	a figure marked on the sides of vessels. The different horizontal

	lines marked on the sides of vessels to indicate the depth to which the vessel can be loaded in different trades.
Preventer	an additional line secured to the outboard end of a boom to prevent the sail and boom from jibing or slating
Ratlines	the rungs of line, iron or wood seized to the shrouds for seamen to use in going aloft
Reach	to sail more broad to the wind than close hauled—close, beam or broad reach
Rotten stuff	the light string-like lashing used to hold a furled sail until ready to break out
Rudder	a swinging fin hanging off the rear of the ship that guides the direction of the vessel. The rudder is attached by ropes and pulleys to the helm.
Run before the wind	to sail with the wind coming over the stern
Running lights	the usual required lights carried when under way
Running rigging	moveable lines in distinction to standing rigging, lines used to control the sails such as halyards, sheets and preventers
Schooner	a fore-and-aft-rigged ship, usually with two masts, built for speed
Scudded	a vessel, seas or clouds running before a gale—scudded along before the force
Scuppers	drains from the waterways

Sheave	the roller in a block or spar over which a line or wire rope passes
Sheer	the upward curve of the deck and rails
Sheets	a line or rope used to control sails
Shrouds	wire cables secured to the masts that return laterally to chain plates near the rails to support the masts
Sibilator	capable of hissing
Slued	to turn or slide sideways or off course; skid
Sole	the bottom or lower deck of a vessel upon which the crew walks, a foundation
Sou'wester	a hat of canvas or oiled cloth with flap at the back worn at sea in stormy weather
Spars	the poles in the ship's rigging—masts, booms, yards, bowsprits, gaffs
Spinnaker	a large, light triangular shaped sail set upon a light spar (spinnaker pole) flown in fair winds
Spreaders	spars jutting from the mast to better stabilize the mast and rigging
Spume	froth or foam on the sea. Frothy matter raised by agitation of the sea.
Squall	a brief, severe storm of wind, usually accompanied by rain and lowered visibility
Starboard quarter aft	the area from abeam to the stern on the right side of a vessel looking forward
Staysail	a triangular fore and aft sail, set from the various stays and named accordingly as the fore topmast staysail

Stern	back of the ship
Storm Trysail	sail of extra heavy canvas for heavy weather use
Stream the log	the act of readying the involved units of the log assembly, should be accomplished to assure its function when streamed to aid navigation.
Tack	the course of a ship sailing close to the wind. Since a sailing ship cannot get closer than 45 degrees off the wind, she sails against the wind by "tacking" or "beating",— sailing on one tack, then coming about on to the other tack
Taffrail	the very after rail of a vessel
Thwart	seat in a small boat
Topping lift	a tackle by which the after or outer end of a boom is hoisted
Top hamper	the upper rigging, masts, spars of a vessel, hence windage in a violent wind
Tracking	to move in the same track as that which precedes, i.e. alignment with towing vessel
Transom	the flat after end or stern of a vessel
Trim	pulling the sheets to adjust the angle of the spars to the direction of the wind
Trysail	a small, heavy triangular sail used fore and aft usually fit at the mainmast without a boom for use in extreme weather to sail by or lie hove to
Unctuous	oily, greasy
Walty	odd, unnatural motion—uneasy

Way	in motion, making progress over the bottom
Ways	a vessel hauls out of the water on tracks and cradle (marine railway)
Whisker pole	a light spar for holding or winging out a headsail before the wind
Whisker shrouds	chains or cables which support a bowsprit laterally
Wildcat	the part of a windlass around which the anchor chain leads. It revolves to bring in or let out the anchor
Windlass	a mechanism variously operated by power or manually using ratchet and brake to turn the drum or wildcat in the process of anchoring
Windward	on the side or direction from which the wind is blowing

Quick Order Form

 e-mail orders: *orders@xlibris.com*

 telephone orders: Call 1-(888) 795-4274

 fax orders: 1-(215) 599-0114

 postal orders: Xlibris
                436 Walnut Street, 11th Floor
                Philadelphia, PA 19106

Please send _____copies of "Sea-Quences"

Name:_____

Address:_____

City:_____State:_____Zip:_____

Payment: ☐ Cheque ☐ Credit Card:
           ___Mastercard ___Visa ___American Express

Card number:_____

Name on Card:_____Exp.Date:_____

Signature:_____ Zip Code: _____